THE 74th ANNUAL
Writer's Digest Writing Competition

Winners

THE GRAND-PRIZE AND

FIRST-PLACE MANUSCRIPTS

IN EACH CATEGORY OF

THE 74TH ANNUAL

WRITER'S DIGEST

WRITING COMPETITION

90066 • *Writer's Digest* • 4700 East Galbraith Road • Cincinnati, OH 45236

These are works of fiction and nonfiction. As applicable, the events and characters described here are imaginary and are not intended to refer to specific places or living persons. The opinions expressed in this manuscript are solely the opinions of the author and do not represent the opinions or thoughts of the publisher or *Writer's Digest*.

The 74th Annual *Writer's Digest* Writing Competition Collection
All Rights Reserved
Copyright © 2005 *Writer's Digest* magazine

The selections printed herein reflect the authors' original manuscripts as submitted to the 74th Annual *Writer's Digest* Writing Competition.

This book may not be reproduced, transmitted, or stored in whole or in part by any means, including graphic, electronic, or mechanical without the express written consent of the publisher except in the case of brief quotations embodied in critical articles and reviews.

Outskirts Press
http://www.outskirtspress.com

ISBN-10: 1-59800-140-X
ISBN-13: 978-1-59800-140-2

Outskirts Press and the "OP" logo are trademarks belonging to Outskirts Press, Inc.

Printed in Canada

INTRODUCTION

The editors of *Writer's Digest* are pleased to share with you the winning entries in each category of the 74th Annual *Writer's Digest* Writing Competition, along with the Grand Prize-winning non-rhyming poem, "White Birch," by Nancy Tupper Ling.

A special thanks goes to our esteemed panel of final-round judges:

- **Nancy Bilyeau** (Feature Article) is an articles editor at *Ladies' Home Journal*. She's also been an editor on the staff of *Good Housekeeping*, *Rolling Stone*, *Men's Journal*, *Healthy Living*, *Mademoiselle* and *American Film*. She wrote a chapter for Therese J. Borchard's *The Imperfect Mom: Candid Confessions of Mothers Living in the Real World*, to be published by Broadway in April 2006.
- **Nancy Breen** (Rhyming Poetry) has judged poetry contests for *Personal Journaling*, *miller's pond*, *Pennwriters* and *The Cincinnati Celtic World Festival*. Her recent chapbooks include *Rites and Observances* (Finishing Line Press) and *How Time Got Away* (Pudding House Publications). She also edits *Poet's Market* for Writer's Digest Books.
- **Aron Eli Coleite** (Stage Play) writes for the NBC forensic drama *Crossing Jordan*. He recently crossed the border of reality in writing/producing *Urban Arcana*, a new TV series for the Sci-Fi Channel based on the Hasbro role-playing game. His play *The Family Room* recently garnered Critic's Choice from *Backstage West* and *LA Weekly*.
- **Jerry B. Jenkins** (Inspirational) is a novelist (the *Left Behind* series), biographer (Hank Aaron, Walter Payton, Billy Graham), and marriage and family author (*Hedges: Loving Your Marriage Enough to Protect It* [Crossway]). He's written more than 150 books and owns Jenkins Entertainment—a filmmaking company in Los Angeles—and the Christian Writers Guild.
- **J.A. Konrath** (Genre Short Story) is the author of the Lt. Jacqueline "Jack" Daniels thrillers *Whiskey Sour* and *Bloody Mary* (both Hyperion). His short stories have appeared in many magazines and anthologies.
- **Warren Littlefield** (Television/Movie Script) spent 10 years as president of NBC Entertainment, where he was responsible for the development of such shows as *Seinfeld*, *Friends*, *Will & Grace* and *ER*. He currently heads the Littlefield Company, where he's produced *Do Over* (WB), *Keen Eddie* (FOX), *Like Family* (WB) and *Love, Inc.* (UPN).

- **Carol Moldaw** (Non-rhyming Poetry) is the author of three books of poetry: *The Lightning Field* (Oberlin College Press), winner of the 2002 Field Poetry Prize; *Chalkmarks on Stone* (La Alameda); and *Taken From the River* (Alef-Bet); as well as a chapbook, *Through the Window* (La Alameda). A recipient of a Pushcart Prize and an NEA Creative Writing Fellowship, Moldaw's work has been widely published in journals, including *Chicago Review*, *Colorado Review*, *Conjunctions*, *Denver Quarterly*, *Field*, *The Kenyon Review*, *The New Republic*, *The New Yorker*, *The Paris Review*, *Parnassus*, *Partisan Review*, *The Threepenny Review* and *TriQuarterly*.
- **Gina Ochsner** (Mainstream/Literary Fiction) won the Flannery O'Connor Award for Short Fiction for her first collection of stories, *The Necessary Grace to Fall* (University of Georgia). Her latest collection, *People I Wanted to Be*, was recently published by Houghton Mifflin.
- **Richard Peck** (Children's Fiction) is the first children's writer to receive a National Humanities Medal. He won the 2001 John Newberry Gold Medal for his 30th book, *A Year Down Yonder*. His 2003 book *The River Between Us* won the Scott O'Dell award in historical fiction. He's written a collection of short stories, *Past Perfect, Present Tense*, and the novel *The Teacher's Funeral* (all Dial Books).
- **Heather Sellers** (Memoir/Personal Essay) has taught nonfiction writing for 15 years. Her book *Page After Page* (Writer's Digest Books) assists writers at all levels with their writing practice. She's the author of four other books and recently completed her memoir, *Face First*.

We'd also like to acknowledge our first-round judges, who evaluated more than 18,000 entries: **Wendy Beckman** (Feature Article), **Liza Burby** (Children's Fiction), **Chad Gervich** (Television/Movie Script), **G. Miki Hayden** (Inspirational Writing), **Patricia Lockwood** (Rhyming Poetry), **Jeffrey Marks** (Genre Short Story), **Debby Mayne** (Mainstream/Literary Short Story), **Dawn Simonds Ramirez** (Memoir/Personal Essay), **Miriam Sagan** (Non-rhyming Poetry) and **Aury Wallington** (Stage Play).

Finally, our most heartfelt congratulations to the winners and to the entrants in this year's competition. The quality of your entries makes the judging more difficult each year. We look forward to seeing your work in the 75th Annual *Writer's Digest* Writing Competition collection.

TABLE OF CONTENTS

Grand-Prize Winner
WHITE BIRCH — NANCY TUPPER LING ... 4

Children's Fiction Winner
TILT — PEGGY TROMBLAY ... 5

Feature Article Winner
FDA PHYSICIAN LEAVES HER MARK ON HISTORY — LINDA BREN ... 10

Genre Short Story Winner
DUET FOR FLUTE AND PHANTOM — MARGARET E. ANDERSON ... 15

Inspirational Winner
IS THIS THE WORLD? — MAL KING ... 24

Mainstream/Literary Short Story Winner
STAINED — TERESA LITTLE ... 29

Memoir/Personal Essay Winner
EDDIE — LORI LOSON ... 36

Non-rhyming Poetry Winner
MY WOMAN — CHRISTO PRETORIUS ... 39

Rhyming Poetry Winner
BACKWARDS THROUGH WET GRASS — ANNA EVANS ... 40

Stage Play Winner
THE SEQUENCE — PAUL MULLIN ... 41

Television/Movie Script Winner
OFF THE FOB — CATHERINE ROSS ... 61

Grand-Prize Winner

WHITE BIRCH

NANCY TUPPER LING
Walpole, MA

A bride among groomsmen,
you stand light and white
against a late November sky.
Oaks and evergreens attend
to you, shield your beauty.
The harsh breeze peels
your papery ribbons like sheets
of *shoji*, bouquets of fallen bark.
Your skin is *yuzen*, the way
your inner bark, once exposed,
emerges inky and black.
    I want to ask: do you know
the family at your woods end?
So many ruthless winters
still: their daughter has grown
tall and striking like you.
Her secrets fall silent,
icicles in snow. I wonder,
will she hear you whisper
wait until spring; wait to find
the flowers inside your catkins,
to watch the scaly spikes drop off.

Children's Fiction Winner

TILT

PEGGY TROMBLAY
Dousman, WI

Me and Eddie raced into Morty's and were on our stools at the counter before the door chimes stopped jingling. It was only 3:30.

I slapped my day's earnings on the counter and started counting it while Eddie rifled around in his pockets.

I'd just tell Pa people refused to work me today in this sweltering July heat. And I'd use the word *sweltering* too, because that's what the adults complained about as I pedaled their errands through Chicago's streets all day.

Eddie elbowed me and grinned at the sweaty coins glistening on the counter. "Wow, Buster. You done pretty good, huh?"

I shrugged. "$2.50 ain't bad." Truth was, I probably could've made a mint.

People were only too happy to have some desperate kid do their work for them. But, I wouldn't give Pa the pleasure of knowing anyone thought like he did. Me and Ma knew different.

I jammed two-bucks worth of change in my pocket. "On account of you helping me, I'm buying today."

Eddie grinned.

"Well look what the heat dragged in." Margie rose from beneath the counter, dropped her sponge in a bucket and wiped her hands in her apron. Margie reminded me of Ma before Pa went to war—cheerful and full of life. In her yellow and white checkered uniform, she strolled toward us as her reflection in the mirror sauntered alongside. "My two favorite customers!" she teased, cupping our chins.

The sweltering heat didn't hurt her none. Sweating made her even prettier.

Eddie pulled back. "Awe, cut that out, Margie."

But I lingered, staring into her marble blue eyes and inhaling her rosy smell.

"I think somebody's got a little heat stroke." She giggled and mussed my hair. "Or has having that handsome mug of yours in the paper gone to your head?"

I winced. Me and Eddie mugging and hugging our favorite pinball machine, Lady Robinhood, had hit the front page of the *Chicago Tribune* on Sunday. Pa was angrier than that ugly stray Maddog that roams

5

Wabash St.

"We'd like a couple of your Chili Dogs," I said and slid forty cents forward.

Eddie piped up, "And we'll earn our shakes."

Margie's smile melted. "Afraid not," she said, clamping her hands on our heads and turning them.

Lady Robinhood was draped in a raggedy white sheet.

"Awe man," Eddie complained. "Is she broke?"

"I bet I could fix her," I said, hopping off my seat.

"Buster, it's not broke," Margie said. "Morty covered it because he doesn't want any more negative publicity."

"That stupid newspaper!" Eddie slammed his fist on the counter. "They've gone and taken our only fun away!"

We'd thought that photographer snapped our picture because I'd just earned the highest score ever on that machine. Instead, we became the poster children for the headline: **Gambling Machines Corrupt Our Young**.

The man down the counter lifted his gaze from his coffee cup and stared at me with a look of recognition.

I climbed back onto my stool. "But the pinball ban doesn't start until Saturday. It's Tuesday. This ain't fair, Margie."

"Try and understand, Buster. Morty's afraid the Mayor's going to march in here wielding a hammer and make an example out of that machine. He's been desperately trying to get rid of it ever since the story hit."

"We ain't gamblers," Eddie grumbled.

"We just want to play pinball," I said. "There's nothing illegal about having fun, is there?"

Eddie's eyes lit up. "Is it because you give us those free shakes? Cuz, if that's the reason, we won't accept 'em no more. Right, Buster?" He poked me.

"Yeah, right."

Margie patted our arms. "Fellas, it's about the law, not shakes." She turned and clipped our order on the cook's wheel. "Johnny, two Chili's!"

"Let 'em play, Miss."

We all stared down the counter toward the gravelly voice.

The stocky man, hunkering over his cup peered out from beneath his hat and pointed at me. "That boy's got a point. There's nothing the mayor can legally do until Saturday. Just let 'em have some fun while they can." He laid down a dollar bill. "And give 'em whatever they want. On me."

Me and Eddie glanced at each other and grinned. I didn't know the man, but I took an instant liking to him.

"Three against one, Margie," cheered Eddie, starting to slide off his stool waiting for her go ahead. "Just say the word."

"Just one game, Margie. We'll cover it right back up," I begged.

She glared at the man. "Now look what you've done. Morty wouldn't—"

"Why don't you let me have a look at this troublemaker first." He eased off his stool, limped over to Lady Robinhood and yanked the sheet off. He ran his fingers over the machine, examining every inch. "You say he wants to sell?" he asked.

Margie's voice softened. "I believe he does."

"She's in nice shape," he said, stroking the glass like it was made of silk. "Have Morty call me. Rocco. Rocco Sincatta." He pulled his card and a couple of nickels from his pocket and set them down on the glass top with a clink. "Enjoy it while you can, boys." He tipped his hat to Margie and smiled. "Now you can blame me."

The door chimes jingled and he disappeared into the blistering heat.

Margie shook her fist at the door. "You can bet your chubby bottom I will."

I fetched his card for Margie. "I like this Rocco guy."

"Give me that!" She snatched his card from me. "Don't go liking that troublemaker."

Eddie's voice floated out from under the machine. "Can I plug her in now?"

I prayed my hands and batted my eyes at Margie. "Can we? Puhlease?"

Margie blew her bangs off her forehead, acting all exhausted like. She wagged her finger at me and scolded, "One game!"

"Seeing Rocco left two nickels," I said, "You mean one game a piece right?"

I jumped back, missing her towel snap by an inch. "Okay. Okay. One game it is."

"Don't push your luck with me, Mister!"

"Thanks, Margie." I blew her a kiss. "Plug her in Eddie!"

Margie threw her hands up and stormed into the kitchen. "I'm pretending I don't know a thing. And when I come back out, that machine better be covered up like nothing happened!" The swinging door banged and fluttered in her wake.

Lady Robinhood blinked to life.

I held the nickel out to Eddie. "You wanna play?"

"Me? Waste our last chance to beat the game? No way, man!" Eddie slapped my back. "You're the man."

I took a deep breath and plugged the nickel in. Lady Robinhood chimed and dinged. Her arrow began flashing as if it were streaking into the air. It was official now.

I was disobeying Pa. His anger from Sunday was still bouncing around in my head. "Is THIS how you're spending your days? Is this what you call WORKING?"

He'd banned me from pinball, but he also forced me and Ma to work while he laid around. So how fair was that? It wasn't.

The bumpers twinkled in a parade of lights. The silver ball materialized, waiting for my electric touch.

I pulled the plunger and the ball blurred its way up around the curve at the top of the machine. It racked up points as it ricocheted between the bumpers. The blaze of lights energized me.

I'm a kid. And kids are supposed to have fun before they grow up. Pa wasn't in his right mind. He was trying to make me skip this fun part.

I watched, waiting for the ball to roll down so I could catch it with my flipper and then aim.

Pinball was a lot like life. It took skill to win. Lots of practice to learn the secrets.

The ball wound its way down the table and I caught it in the crook of my right flipper and tapped the button. I propelled it up and away, on another trip bouncing around the table.

You needed to plan your game—aim for those high-point bumpers. Sorta like what me and Ma were doing with Pa. He was that gap between the flippers where the ball was heading. I gently shoved the table to the right and the ball jerked off course. You had to know how to shake things up enough to steer the ball, but avoid the tilt. We'd learned to work around him these past couple years. But sometimes still, no matter how hard I tried, that ball would just slip down the middle and end the game. Like Pa's over-reaction to that *Tribune* picture on Sunday.

I raised the flippers and caught the ball again. Knowing how far to let the ball roll down the flipper before flicking was my specialty. I could aim like no one else.

"Hey Buster." Eddie yelled, knowing that's the only way I'd hear him. "Johnny brought our dogs out. Ya want me to bring it over?"

I shook him off. "Nah. What's my score?" I asked, never taking my eye off the ball.

"100,000. Keep going Buster!"

Eddie's cheers faded away. The bumpers chimed and dinged with every touch.

It suddenly smelled like someone rolled the garbage wagon from the alley, inside.

"Eddie! Put your shoes back on man!" I yelled. "You're stinkin' up the place."

Someone walked up beside me. I figured it was Eddie again. But then, that someone shoved the machine. The "Tilt" alarm buzzed and Lady Robinhood fell dark and silent!

Anger charged through my body. "What are ya doing!? I was right in—"

Tank, the neighborhood's nightmare, lunged forward, thrusting his face in mine and growled, "Are you yelling at me?"

The sweltering heat was obviously not his friend. I stepped backwards out of his stink.

He stepped forward. Angry beads of sweat marched down his temples.

Eddie bobbed in and out of sight behind Tank's shoulders, frantically waving his hands to warn me. As if I needed reminding of our last encounter.

I backed into a chair and froze, fearing one of Tank's over-ripe pimples would blow any second and blind me.

"You better not be," he snarled as a dribble of Chili bounced down his chin, "Or I'll scrub the street with you. Again." Tank thumbed the blame. "Orders from the counter."

Eddie scurried back to his stool.

Margie stood with her hands parked on her hips. "That's enough there, or I'll be handing YOU the mop, Theodore."

Tank cringed.

Theodore? I bit my lip to keep from laughing. I think Margie had a little bit of gangster blood in her. Only she could get away with calling a wise-guy by his real name.

She aimed her finger at me. "And Buster. Game's over. Cover it up." This was the Margie that meant business.

Tank lumbered away toward the counter and I picked up the sheet and covered Lady Robinhood.

"You would've beat her Buster," Eddie whispered as I plopped onto my stool. "I know it."

I reached for my dog and stopped, staring at the big chunk missing. Then I remembered Tank's chin and pushed my plate away.

Tank reached over and nabbed it. "I'll take that."

"And that'll be twenty cents," Margie said, gently whacking him upside the head. "Should I have Johnny make you another, Buster?"

"Nah. I sorta lost my appetite." I sneered at Tank.

"Ah, get over yourself. You ain't so hot," Tank sputtered, spewing bits of dog. "I could beat ya."

"All this tough guy talk is exhausting me." Margie grabbed her bucket and paused at the kitchen door. "Don't make me come back out here and show you who's really boss." She raised one of her velvety eyebrows at Tank. "Got me?"

Nobody could resist Margie's charm. Not even Tank. We all smiled.

"Good," she said and vanished into the kitchen.

(EXCERPT FROM A MIDDLE-GRADE NOVEL)

Feature Article Winner

FDA PHYSICIAN LEAVES HER MARK ON HISTORY

LINDA BREN
Portland, OR

It was early 1942 and war was raging in the jungles of the Pacific. In addition to fighting the Japanese, Allied troops found themselves under attack by malaria-carrying mosquitoes. Enemy soldiers had already captured several plantations of cinchona trees, the source of the antimalarial, quinine. So the search was on for a quinine substitute to combat the disease.

A possible treatment in the form of a dark, inky substance arrived for testing in the pharmacology department at the University of Chicago. Pharmacologist Frances Oldham Kelsey, like many other university researchers throughout the country, had enlisted in the search for malaria cures.

The inky substance had been sent by a veterinarian in Texas. "He said that he had just tried it on his secretary without ill effects," says Kelsey, "and he planned next to try it on cattle. It showed the relative value placed on women and cattle in Texas at that time."

The war ended without finding a good substitute for quinine. But Kelsey did learn something valuable from the experience. She learned that rabbits metabolized quinine rapidly, but pregnant rabbits had less ability to break down the drug, and embryonic rabbits could not break it down at all. She also learned that drugs could pass through the placental barrier between mother and unborn child. These insights would serve Kelsey well some 15 years later when in 1960, as a new Food and Drug Administration employee, she was asked to evaluate a drug most thought was harmless. That drug was thalidomide.

Although pressured by the manufacturer to quickly approve a drug already in widespread use throughout the rest of the world, Kelsey held her ground. When she repeatedly asked for more safety data and forestalled the approval of thalidomide, Kelsey did more than keep a dangerous drug off the market. She set into motion a series of events that would forever change the way drugs are tested, evaluated, and introduced in America.

The Thalidomide Tragedy

All they wanted was a good night's sleep, and thalidomide gave it to them. It brought a quick, natural sleep for millions of people with insomnia, and it also gave pregnant women relief from morning sickness. The drug's German manufacturer claimed it was non-addictive, caused no hangover, and was safe for pregnant women. And, unlike barbiturates, its lack of toxicity made it a poor choice for a suicide attempt.

By 1960, thalidomide was sold throughout Europe and South America, in Canada, and in many other countries. To sell it in the United States, the Richardson-Merrell pharmaceutical company of Cincinnati submitted an application to FDA in September 1960.

The application was assigned to medical officer Kelsey, who had joined FDA just one month earlier. It was her first drug review assignment.

Under the law at that time, FDA had 60 days to review a drug application. If an FDA medical officer notified the company that the application was incomplete, it was considered withdrawn and the company would have to resubmit it with additional data. With each resubmission, the 60-day clock would start again.

Kelsey had concerns about the drug from the beginning. So did the pharmacologist and chemist who assisted her. "We were concerned about the non-absorption," says Kelsey. "That you could give enormous amounts, both to animals and humans, without toxicity. We felt that there might be conditions, illnesses, or other drugs that might change the absorption, and toxic effects might appear." After Kelsey detailed the deficiencies in a letter to Richardson-Merrell, the company sent in additional information—but not enough to satisfy her.

"The clinical reports were more on the nature of testimonials," says Kelsey, "rather than the results of well-designed, well-executed studies."

Kelsey continued to request more safety data, and with each request, the 60-day clock restarted. Dr. Joseph Murray, Richardson-Merrell's representative, grew increasingly frustrated. He complained to Kelsey's superiors that she was nit-picking and delaying the drug's approval unnecessarily.

But Kelsey did not cave.

"I think I always accepted the fact that one was going to get bullied and pressured by industry," says Kelsey. Richardson-Merrell seemed particularly anxious, she says, because Christmas is apparently the season for sleeping pills. "They came right out and said, 'We want to get this drug on the market before Christmas, because that is when our best sales are.'"

In December of 1960, three months after Richardson-Merrell submitted its application, the *British Medical Journal* published a letter from a physician, Leslie Florence, who had prescribed thalidomide to his patients. Florence reported seeing cases of peripheral neuritis, a painful tingling of the arms and feet, in patients who had taken the drug for a long time.

After reading Florence's letter, Kelsey immediately contacted Richardson-Merrell to request further information on this serious side effect. Recalling how quinine had affected adult rabbits and fetuses differently, Kelsey wondered what effects thalidomide may have if used during pregnancy. She suspected that a drug that could damage nerves could also affect a developing fetus.

Her suspicions soon proved to be grimly accurate.

European physicians began reporting a disturbing phenomenon. A growing number of women were giving birth to terribly deformed babies. Some had abnormally short limbs, with toes sprouting directly from the hips, and flipper-like arms. Others had malformed internal organs or eye and ear defects.

At first, no one knew the cause. But a German pediatrician, Widukind Lenz, found that half of the mothers with deformed children he saw as patients had taken thalidomide in the first trimester of pregnancy.

In November 1961, Lenz warned the German manufacturer about the dangers of thalidomide. Ten days later, German health authorities pulled the drug from the market. Other countries closely followed Germany's lead. In March 1962, Richardson-Merrill withdrew its application from FDA.

For many, it was already too late.

More than 10,000 children in 46 countries were estimated to have been born with deformities as a consequence of thalidomide. The damage in the United States was small by comparison, but no less devastating to the 17 children born in America with thalidomide-associated deformities.

Richardson-Merrell had distributed more than 2.5 million thalidomide tablets to more than 1,000 doctors throughout the United States on what was called an investigational basis. The doctors, in turn, gave thalidomide to nearly 20,000 patients, several hundred of whom were pregnant women.

FDA's field staff located the doctors who had been given thalidomide and urged them to contact patients who had been given the drug. But not all of the doctors kept records of the drug's distribution. Through news releases, FDA warned women of the danger of taking the drug, but it is unlikely that all of these women were reached.

Kelsey's Early Career

Canadian-born Kelsey attended McGill University in Montreal and graduated with an M.Sc. in pharmacology in 1935. On her professor's urging, Kelsey wrote to E.M.K. Geiling, M.D. Geiling, a noted researcher, was starting up a pharmacology department at the University of Chicago.

Kelsey was delighted when she read Geiling's letter offering her a research assistantship and scholarship in the Ph.D. program at Chicago. But there was one problem—one that "tweaked my conscience a bit," she says.

The letter began "Dear Mr. Oldham," Oldham being her maiden name. Kelsey asked her professor at McGill if she should wire back and explain that her first name, Frances, with an "e" is female. "Don't be ridiculous," he said. "Accept the job, sign your name, put 'Miss' in brackets afterwards, and go!"

So Kelsey went.

"To this day, I do not know if my name had been Elizabeth or Mary Jane, whether I would have had that first big step up," says Kelsey. "And to his dying day, Professor Geiling would never admit one way or the other."

In 1937, Kelsey's second year at the University of Chicago, FDA asked Geiling to help determine why people were dying after they drank "Elixir Sulfanilamide." Sulfanilamide, introduced in pill-form in 1935, was extremely effective in fighting bacterial infections. But the pills were pretty unpalatable. One manufacturer, the S. E. Massengill Company of Bristol, Tenn., asked its chemist to find a liquid solution in which the drug could be dissolved, making it more pleasant-tasting, especially to children.

"The solution was put right on the market with a little pink coloring and a little cherry flavoring, and it sold like wildfire," says Kelsey. Under the law at that time, the Food and Drugs Act of 1906, a company could sell a drug without showing its safety.

Soon after the elixir hit the market, reports of deaths started flowing in, but no one was sure whether it was the sulfanilamide or the solvent that was poisonous.

As Geiling's assistant, Kelsey helped conduct tests to identify the toxic element. It became apparent that it was the solvent, diethylene glycol, which is similar to antifreeze.

The immediate outcome of Elixir Sulfanilamide was tragic—it caused 107 deaths, many of them in children. It also led to the suicide of Massengill's chemist and to a fine of $26,100 levied against Massengill, the highest that was legally allowed at the time. Since the manufacturer was not required to demonstrate its product's safety, FDA could not hold Massengill accountable for the deaths. The company could only be fined for "misbranding" its product. An elixir, by definition, contained alcohol, but there was no alcohol in Elixir Sulfanilamide.

The long-term effects were also remarkable. Public outrage spurred the passage of the Federal Food, Drug, and Cosmetic Act of 1938. The new drug law required companies to show evidence of safety before their product could be marketed, and warn of the potential hazards of a drug.

Kelsey went on to earn a Ph.D. in pharmacology and an M.D. from the University of Chicago, where she met and married Dr. Fremont Kelsey. She spent the next decade teaching, working as a physician, and raising her two daughters. In 1960, Kelsey left the Midwest to accept a position at FDA in Washington, D.C.

The Road to Stronger Drug Laws

The headline read "'Heroine' of FDA Keeps Bad Drug Off of Market." The story appeared on the front page of The Washington Post on July 15, 1962. Reporter Morton Mintz told "how the skepticism and stubbornness of a Government physician prevented what could have been an appalling American tragedy, the birth of hundreds or indeed thousands of armless and legless children."

Mintz's article catapulted Kelsey to stardom. It also inspired a flurry of follow-up articles on drug control in The New York Times and other mainstream media of the day.

In recognition of Kelsey's vigilance, President John F. Kennedy, on Aug. 17, 1962, presented Kelsey with the highest honor that can be bestowed upon a U.S. civilian: the medal for Distinguished Federal Civilian Service.

The American public came to realize how narrowly they had averted a major tragedy. And politicians who had been fighting for tighter drug controls were finally taken seriously. A controversial bill introduced by Sen. Estes Kefauver of Tennessee several years earlier was resurrected from its congressional committee graveyard and rewritten. President Kennedy signed the bill, generally known as the Kefauver-Harris Amendments, into law on Oct. 10, 1962. This landmark drug law, which modified the earlier Federal Food, Drug, and Cosmetic Act of 1938, changed the way new drugs were regulated.

Under the 1938 law, drug manufacturers had only to show that their drugs were safe. Under the 1962 law, they also had to show that all new drugs were effective. Kelsey was there for both, participating in the creation of two of the most important public health laws in the nation's history.

At 86, Kelsey continues to persevere in safeguarding public health, serving as deputy of scientific and medical affairs in FDA's office of compliance.

"It has been an interesting career," says Kelsey. And of her first drug review assignment at FDA in 1960—the thalidomide application—she notes, "They gave it to me because they thought it would be an easy one to start on. As it turned out, it wasn't all that easy."

Genre Short Story Winner

DUET FOR FLUTE AND PHANTOM

MARGARET E. ANDERSON
Houston, TX

Sensing a presence looming over the wall of my cubicle, I looked up into the handsome face of my new work mate, Connor Crowley. Picture Hugh Grant, a bit more squarely chiseled.

"The closest motel is fifty miles from our site." Connor handed me a printout. "But this place is a stone's throw. What do you think?"

I was breakneck busy and perfectly willing to let Connor choose the accommodations for our field trip. With his exquisite taste, and my substandard standards of a solid roof and no bed bugs, how could we go wrong? I was not, however, willing to cut short a conversation with the new heart throb of the Kiskadee Soil Research Foundation—no matter that the two of us would soon be *a deux* for a whole week in Louisiana.

Scanning the printout, my eyes caught the words, "Bed & Breakfast... plantation...housekeeping cottages...haunted." "Haunted, huh? You bringing your ghost-busting kit?" I asked.

Connor winked one of his ice-blue peepers at me. "Most spirits are benevolent."

"Okay. Let's go for it."

* * *

True to his word, Connor showed up at my house the next morning sans ghost repellents.

He did, however, come loaded for bear, literally, with an I-don't-know-what gauge shotgun so big I couldn't have held it steady, let alone hit anything with it. I take that back. I could hit something if I used the gun as a club, but I didn't plan on getting that close to a bear.

"Bears are extinct in Louisiana, right?" I asked.

"Just because no one's seen them, doesn't mean they aren't around." Connor heaved a suitcase into my trunk. "Look at the ivory billed woodpecker."

I gazed overhead, to left and to right.

"Not here, silly. What I mean is, they've considered that bird extinct for decades. Now there's fresh evidence it still exists."

We were planning to sample soils in undeveloped areas. Wouldn't it be something if we were the ones to spot the rare bird?

I watched as Connor transferred the rest of his gear from his car to

15

mine. Another suitcase, dead weights, camping equipment. "Camping equipment? I thought you booked that B&B."

Connor straightened up, flexing his well-muscled back. "Just in case the car breaks down or we have a change of plans."

I guessed Connor used to be a boy scout 'cause he sure was prepared. He finished up the luggage transfer with a huge ice chest and enough grocery bags to fill the trunk and overflow to the back seat. Not only prepared, but he liked to cook? Connor was beginning to seem too good to be true. So far, I couldn't find a fault.

Not, that is, 'till we had been on the road awhile. In the two hundred fifty miles to our destination, he must have asked me two hundred forty-nine times if I'd like him to drive. I would have written that off as one of those pesky guy things, except that each "No, thanks" was followed by a casual comment, such as, "It's so easy to slip into speeding when you're tired—unconsciously, of course."

In between driving tips, I received plenty of advice on diet and exercise. I wouldn't have taken them personally were Connor not so perfect and I slightly overweight and out of shape.

The more Connor talked, the tighter I clenched the wheel. With one temple throbbing out a prelude to a headache, I mashed the accelerator and blasted ahead. I couldn't wait to escape from that car, even if the evacuation route led to a haunted house. Obviously, road trips were Connor's feet of clay. I'd rather have a ghost join our company and Connor back to his charming self.

* * *

"Nobody's ever seen him..." Our hostess, Vermillion Boudreaux, enthroned in a Queen Anne wing chair, paused her description of the resident ghost to fill our cups from a silver teapot. "But Liam moves things around at night and sometimes plays his flute."

Connor leaned in eagerly, his blue eyes round as the macaroons on his plate. "What a coincidence! Liam's my middle name, and my mother insisted on giving me flute lessons as a child. I wonder what it means?"

I thought it suspiciously convenient that Liam-the-ghost never showed himself. Vermillion might play flute, too, and having free reign of the house, she could certainly shuffle things around overnight. "If no one's ever seen Liam," I asked, "how do you know he's male?"

"It's the things he does, *chere*. Liam was the old plantation butler. He tidies up at night. Once he brought me a bouquet of azaleas. Even put them in a porcelain vase."

"That is amazing," I said dryly.

Vermillion obviously relished telling ghost stories. She dressed the part in a long flowing caftan with dangling jet earrings and necklace—the very picture of the mistress of a haunted house.

Setting her cup daintily in its saucer, she rose to signal the end of her traditional welcome tea. "If y'all are finished, I'll show you to your cottage."

Connor and I trailed her out the back of her ante-bellum home. The spacious backyard was lush with plants and shade trees. I wished I could have seen the azaleas and rhododendrons in full bloom, but the oleanders more than made up for that. Lining the back and one side of the yard, they sported more hues than I'd ever seen in one place—white, yellow, peach, and a half dozen shades of pink and red. Dark ivy climbed the latticed sides of a white gazebo.

In a break between the oleanders, I saw a gate in the back fence, and on the other side, a thicket.

"Do you own those woods?" I asked.

"Some of them, *chere*. I have foot trails y'all can explore. My property ends at another fence farther back."

Connor and I exchanged a glance, and I knew we were thinking the same thing—a great place to take soil samples.

Vermillion led us to a broad, squat outbuilding and unlocked the door, handing each of us a key. "This was the kitchen, back when having one in the big house was a fire hazard."

"And your other cottage used to be the carriage house?" Connor asked.

"That's right, *cher*. Y'all let me know if you need anything." Vermillion left us to unload and settle in.

The original building must have included quarters for the kitchen staff, for we each had a small bedroom in addition to our sitting room, with a modern kitchenette running along one side.

As I took my time unpacking, my headache began to wane. Emerging from my room, I plopped into a puffy chintz easy chair and gazed out at Vermillion's woods. Ah! The country sounds of birds and bugs—and Connor reciting the inventory of each food item he unpacked, along with its *raison d'etre*.

"Plenty of fresh veggies and fruit so we don't need synthetic vitamins. Chamomile and ginger tea—natural expectorant. Yogurt's good for the bowels."

I was beginning to have the sinking feeling that Connor's feet of clay extended all the way up to his knees.

"Fat-free cottage cheese, fat-free rye crackers, fat-free popcorn."

When Connor smiled across the bar, I got the distinct impression he focused his baby blues on my thighs, which contrasted distinctly with his fat-free bod. As he resumed his food litany, I stumped away for another hit of aspirin.

By the time I returned, Connor had finished unpacking, and therefore, reciting, thank heaven. I leaned my head back in the chair and closed my eyes.

Clunk, thunk, bash, bang.

Now what? I hauled myself to the kitchenette where Connor removed

17

assorted cooking utensils from drawers and cabinets to the counter. Handing me a spoon, he said, "Feel how greasy that is." He started hot water running in the sink.

"What are you going to make?"

"Scratch biscuits—with canola oil, not butter."

I intended to help with the cooking, but couldn't do much until he cleared the tiny counter. Poking around the pantry, I found a jar of honey. "This will taste good on those biscuits."

"Let's see."

I held the jar in front of Connor's face, since his hands were submerged in soapy water.

"You'd eat that?"

"I thought honey was good for you."

"That kind could have been made from non-organic pollen."

Lowering my eyebrows, I grabbed the allegedly greasy spoon, downed a big gulp of honey, then retired to my room again.

After firmly shutting the door, I tried to collect my thoughts. Connor was driving himself nuts. So why was my heart pounding in time with the throbbing of my headache?

Maybe I was mad at myself. What kind of dunce could have thought this guy was attractive? When I recalled all the times I've criticized men who can't see past a mop of bottle blond hair and a Barbie chest, my head pounded harder. Mentally picturing Connor's face, I now saw murky gray eyes, not blue; a narrower chin; one slightly crooked tooth.

Perhaps I could have tolerated Connor's habits were it not for his constant proselytizing about them. It seemed everything he did had a nitpicking protocol. And every nitpick that flashed through his mind popped out of his mouth. It was as if I were inside Connor's brain with him, torturing myself with all his compulsive thoughts.

One thing was certain. I had to calm down. Connor and I had a week's work to do—together. I put on a tape of soothing classical music and tried self nurturing. *I am not stupid*, I said to myself. *I couldn't have known about Connor's anal-retentive life style just by working in the same office for a few weeks.* I meditated to the mantra, *I am in control*, 'till the tape ended, then rose, pasted on a smile, and went out to join Connor for supper.

I had to admit the biscuits were good. I promised to reciprocate later with my special peach cobbler.

After we ate, Connor said, "Want to get a few samples from these woods before dark?"

"You bet! Give me a sec to get ready." That's what we needed—fresh air and exercise.

Connor passed me going into the bathroom as I came out. A few moments later, he appeared in my room. "I took out a bar of soap for me," he said. "Mine's on the left side of the sink. Yours is on the right. You are right-handed, aren't you?"

"Why can't we both—"

"More sanitary."

He arranged the throw pillows on my bed in a perfectly symmetrical pattern, then left to change his shoes.

A wicked image appeared in my mind's eye. An image of me holding one of those pillows against Connor's face 'till he stopped moving. In consideration of his superior physical strength, I shook off my vision and rearranged the pillows as asymmetrically as possible.

After changing into my hiking boots, I went to the back door where I found Connor wearing gloves and a full body suit of mosquito netting, complete with a veil hanging from his hat brim. He stared disapprovingly at my shorts and tee shirt. "You're not going out like that, are you?"

Hard to answer through the viselike clenching of my teeth. "Why not?" squeezed out.

"How many insect-borne diseases do you want to attract? West Nile, St. Louis encephalitis, Lyme disease—"

"Excuse me a moment." I slipped back to the bathroom to switch the bars of soap to opposite sides of the sink.

* * *

In time, our trek through the peaceful woods improved my mood. Birds sang their bedtime lullabies. Bees buzzed. Gathering samples turned our conversation from soap and disease to the sorts of things we talked about at the office—back when Connor was still good-looking. As we returned to the cottage at dusk, the bird songs evolved into night noises—crickets, frogs, a screech owl.

So mellow did I feel that I said, "You take a load off while I whip up that peach cobbler I was telling you about."

"Oh, right, your special family recipe. I can't wait."

I'd bought the peaches from a roadside stand—juicy, tree ripe, Texas Hill County peaches, not those mealy supermarket things. Only the best for my cobbler.

Instead of resting while I cooked, Connor appeared by my warm side as soon as I began to assemble my ingredients, eager to learn my culinary secrets.

"I wish we had some ice cream for your cobbler," he mused, "or even coffee cream."

"Won't need it on this puppy." My chin lifted with pride. "I don't overpower my special spices and light pastry with any toppings."

While I peeled one peach, Connor picked up another, sniffed it. "Are these organic?"

Somehow, I managed to complete the project without kicking Connor out of the kitchen. Once the sweet, homey scent began to fill the room, he seemed to settle down. We watched a little TV. Then, when I took the cobbler from the oven, Connor poured himself a glass of milk.

"I'd like milk, too," I told him.

"Chocolate or white?"

Whipping my head around, I saw that he was stirring chocolate syrup into his glass.

"White, of course. Chocolate doesn't go with peach cobbler."

Connor shrugged and carried the two glasses to the table while I served up the desert. I'd no sooner set his bowl down than, before my incredulous eyes, he proceeded to pour his chocolate milk over his cobbler.

"Oh, no! You've ruined it." My horrified cry filled the small room.

Connor waved his hand dismissively. "What's the big deal? It all goes down the same chute. I had no idea you were so picky!"

My next howl was incoherent, the primal kind that erupts from the gut.

"Get a grip," said Connor. "Relax."

Flinging myself into a chair, I took a bite of cobbler. *King Compulsive the First called* me *picky?* The thought almost canceled out the taste of spiced peaches. Almost, but not quite. The next bite tasted even better. I ate all I could, not only because the cobbler was so good, but also to prevent Connor from defiling more of it with chocolate milk. Feeling better, I decided to retire before Connor could upset me again.

Yet, once in bed, my raw nerves flared, daring me to fall asleep. *Where does* he *get off telling* me *to relax?* Every negative emotion known to Dr. Phil and Stephen King coursed through my veins. The one that finally stuck was indignation. And I was ready to relish that righteous indignation, nurture it, wallow in it, even if I didn't sleep a wink.

But I couldn't relish it. Other problems drove my high horse right out of the barn in my brain.

Was that a grunt I heard outside? A shuffling noise? Could there be bears in the woods after all?

I slipped out of bed and peeked through the curtains. Saw nothing. Could it be the ghost?

Curled under the sheet again, I began to doubt myself, and the more I did so, the more I resented Connor.

Did bears and spirits walk? Did bears have ticks? Ticks with Lyme disease? Deer had them.

Were there deer in Vermillion's woods?

Lyme disease, encephalitis, West Nile—they were serious diseases, and it would be just my luck to contract one of them. Could I really get cancer from non-organic foods? *Nonsense!* All these wild thoughts were Connor's doing.

A few hours ago, hours that seemed like years, I'd been able to joke about this, at least mentally. I'd thought of *The Odd Couple,* Felix and Oscar. But I wasn't really a thoughtless slob like Oscar. Was I? My sisters seemed to think I was too finicky.

But then... What if... Oh, God. When my sisters said "finicky," was that a euphemism for "pain in the posterior"? The idea that I might make others feel the way Connor made me feel raised my discomfort to a whole new level. I would have gone looking for Connor's shotgun, but I figured it was so big that, once I got the business end into my mouth, my short, fat, out of shape arms wouldn't reach the trigger.

Finicky? Picky? Could Connor, of all people, possibly be right about me?

No! I shook my head so hard my brain bounced against my skull. *No. No. No.* It was Connor who was off base, way beyond left field, beyond the ball park, and even beyond Felix Unger.

Distraction, that's what I needed. I got up and hooked my notebook computer to the phone line, fiddled around on the Internet awhile, researching some of the flora and fauna I'd seen here at Vermillion's. At 3 a.m., I climbed back in bed and fell into a restless sleep.

Nevertheless, I was up before Connor the next day. I went for a ramble in the woods, first donning jeans, long-sleeved shirt and hat, and dosing my face and hands with DEET.

Nature in the predawn cool, the smell of dew-moistened foliage, the first stirrings of waking wildlife, all soothed my soul. The more I relaxed, the more details I noticed—some pretty orange mushrooms, a beehive in a hollow tree, a long procession of ants crossing the trail.

By the time I got back to the cottage, I felt so much better I thought I might be able to nod off for awhile, but Connor was waiting for me. The minute I crossed the threshold, he called from his room, "You've got to see this!" When I entered, he gestured to the top of the chest of drawers. "Liam's been here."

"Looks the same to me." Neat and symmetrical as everything else in Connor's room.

"This wasn't here before." Connor pointed to a small porcelain plate bearing a couple of fine Belgian chocolates wrapped in gold foil.

"Is that all? Vermillion probably left them."

"If she had, she'd have given you some, too."

"Maybe I'm not the right gender to get chocolates from Vermillion." I winked. But Connor did have a point. "I was up most of the night, and I didn't hear anyone come in," I conceded thoughtfully. "But whoever brought the candy is gone, and now I have something to show you before breakfast."

I led Connor back into the woods, determined to astound him with my skill in finding mushrooms and other natural wonders.

But no matter how tiny my balloon, Connor seemed determined to burst it. He knew the full Latin name of my orange mushrooms—*Boletus Rufus, Bloatus Regurgus*, something like that. Moreover, he found five other species I'd missed. There was one he couldn't name—wonder of wonders! While he riffled through his *Field Guide to Fungi*—no small feat in his thick gloves, I strode ahead.

When Connor caught up with me, I stood transfixed, listening. Amidst the bird calls and wind-rustled leaves ran a faint strain of flute music.

It was not my imagination. Connor heard it, too. "I told you Liam was trying to communicate with us," he said.

It didn't seem to surprise Connor that Liam turned out a virtuoso performance worthy of James Galway. Like a kid after the Pied Piper, he followed the music to the very thing I'd meant to show him, the bee hive. If I'd believed in Liam, I might have said he was in league with Connor to steal my thunder.

Connor clapped his gloved hands in ecstasy. "Natural, organic honey. You see, Liam is benevolent. He led us to this hive."

"How do you know it's organic?" I groused.

"I researched the area. There's no agriculture for miles and miles."

"Fine," I snapped. "But how do you propose to get it without being stung."

Connor flapped his veil and the arms of his bug suit. "This isn't ordinary mosquito netting. It's bee proof. Can't be too careful with the Africanized species spreading through the countryside."

Well, I wasn't wearing a bee suit, and what he stirred up could take its revenge on me. With a disgusted puff, I left him to it. As I hared back to the cottage, I swore I would not eat his superior honey. In fact, I made a point of taking the jar from the pantry and eating from it right in front of him when he returned with his organic honeycombs.

Thus I instigated a honey-gulping war. We matched each other slurp for slurp, biscuit for biscuit, Connor determined to lead me down the straight and narrow honey path, and I equally determined to show him the store-bought stuff was harmless. By the time I reached the bottom of my jar, all I could do was loll around like Jabba the Hut, no doubt confirming Connor's opinion of my inferior state of health.

* * *

Standing beside me in the bay window of her living room, Vermillion chewed the polish off a long, red fingernail. We watched a khaki-clad sheriff walk from his cruiser to the front door.

When Vermillion let him in, I was relieved to see that his face wasn't as grim as the last time he'd been here. Vermillion must have seen the improvement, too, for she abandoned her nervous nail mangling.

"Sit down, sheriff," she said. "I hope you have good news, or, good as it can be under the circumstances?"

The officer remained standing but smiled. "Miz Boudreaux," he said, "it wasn't murder."

Tears of relief shone in Vermillion's eyes. "Then what killed him?"

Turning his Stetson over in his hands, the man drawled, "It was that wild honey he ate. Made from the pollen of azaleas, rhododendrons and oleanders, and poison like the flowers themselves."

Vermillion gasped and fell into her throne-like chair. I hurried to her side, and she clutched my hand. "*Chere*, I'm so glad we didn't eat any. We could have died, too."

"Maybe. But Connor had an awful lot of it." With a wistful smile I recalled our honey-eating contest.

The sheriff nodded solemnly, then said to me, "You're free to go on home, ma'am."

* * *

I loaded the car, ready to take the sheriff's advice and "go on home." My small tape player, I put in the trunk. After all, I had one built into the dash, on which I listened to my tape of James Galway on flute all the way home. After unpacking, I nestled into my ratty but comfy recliner and polished off the rest of my fine Belgian chocolates wrapped in gold foil.

Tonight, I thought, *I will sleep deep.*

I didn't. Flute music woke me in the dead of night. At first I thought I'd left the stereo on, but with a sick lurch of my stomach, I realized that I didn't own any recordings of the tune that wafted through my house.

Leaping from the bed, I snapped on the light to see that all the items on my dresser had been rearranged with compulsively perfect symmetry.

Inspirational Winner

IS THIS THE WORLD?
MAL KING
Santa Paula, CA

Dogs are not our whole life, but they make our lives whole.
—Roger Caras

Aspen, Colorado 1959

"Daddy, is this...is this the world?"
Debbie, my seven-year-old daughter, gazes around at the fairy-tale town of Aspen and waits for my answer.
Like her, I'm awed by Aspen's splendor: five-color Victorian houses, slant sunlight, golden aspen throbbing against the sky's blue vigor. Here to buy her a doll for her birthday, I rush around and open the car door for her. In the alpine coolness of early fall when life and death seem most aware of each other, she takes my hand and I feel taller, more alive.
"Thanks, Daddy." Looking in wonderment at Ajax Mountain, she squeezes my hand and repeats her question.
How to answer her? My family and I are vacationing with my parents who live in nearby Basalt. I needed this retreat after helping prosecute Ma Duncan—a notorious woman who hired two assassins to kill her daughter-in-law, nine-months pregnant. I pull myself back from the murder case and again savor the breathless scenery that prompted Debbie to ask the question. She'll soon know about that other world; right now I want to protect her.
"Yes, this is the world."
She stumbles on the sidewalk and would have fallen except for my hand. A young blonde in a yellow dress strolls out of an ice cream store, gives Debbie a sympathetic look.
"May I have an ice cream *and* a doll, Daddy?"
Inside the store, I get a minor shock. A cone costs almost as much as a quart in California. Debbie orders a double-dip Neapolitan. Conscious of our budget, I don't order anything. I take her hand and we walk to downtown Aspen to look for a toy store. Debbie has just finished her ice cream when she spots a pet store.
"Oh, boy! Daddy, could I have a puppy instead of a doll?"
She'd been heartbroken when a car had killed her German shepherd. "Sure," I say, already worrying about whether our budget can afford an Aspen puppy.

"Will you let me buy the dog I want?"

Surprised by the question, I glance down at her. "Sure, hon. Why are you frowning?"

"Mommy says you buy the first thing you see."

Debbie has touched on the one point of conflict in my marriage. I buy. Regina shops.

"You're so special, I'll stay while you shop."

Blue-grey eyes search mine as Debbie's leg braces click. "Isn't Mommy special?"

More special than words can capture.

I glance at my watch. In an hour and a half, I'm to meet a publisher interested in my book proposal about the Ma Duncan case. Eager to get Debbie what she wants and still make the meeting, I open the store door for her. A bell chimes and we're in an echo chamber full of puppies trying to win the prize for shrillness. I take a deep breath, shake my head. This has to be the Tiffany of pet stores: museum-quality wall art, and floral arrangements between row after row of glass-enclosed puppies, scented by dog food and potpourri.

"Thanks for bringing me here, Daddy. This is like a heaven for puppies."

"How about that one?" I ask Debbie as she gets down on her knees, presses her nose against the glass. A cute collie wiggles its tail.

"Daddy, you said you'd let me shop. Your rushing me isn't helping."

An hour passes and I feel sweat roll down my sides. Unless she finds one soon, I'll have time *and* money trouble. Wish I had brought the publisher's number. The farther back into the store we go, the more expensive the puppies. I guess the owner figures that buyers will adjust to the escalating prices. Or pass out. Reminding myself to relax, I sigh, unclench my hands.

"Do you like any of these, Daddy?"

Way out of my price range. Instead of saying that, I shrug and smile at the shop owner, an older woman who looks like she probably owns Aspen and has never done anything more strenuous than shop. Wise enough to stay in the background until a little girl ropes and ties her daddy, she smiles back.

A few minutes later, she says, "What kind of puppy are you looking for?"

Debbie turns, curtsies. "I'll know her when I see her, ma'am."

Because Aspen housing costs are mountain high, my parents bought in Basalt. On old maps, Basalt appears as Fryingpan Junction. According to legend, Ute Indians attacked silver prospectors almost killing one of them. His companions hid him in a cave and marked the spot with a frying pan. I feel as if I'm moving from the frying pan of reasonable prices into the fire of Aspen prices.

A few minutes later, I realize I'm not going to make the meeting

25

unless I leave now. The tension in my arms cranks up several notches. "Maybe we can come back tomorrow."

Debbie strikes a hands-on-hips pose. "Mom warned me about you."

"Your wife has trained her vell." The owner speaks with a European accent.

Five minutes before my scheduled meeting, Debbie asks the storeowner, "Ma'am, you have any more puppies?"

"Just two. In back. One I'm returning because he's puny and the other just came in and is the most expensive breed I stock."

My heart sinks as I follow Vell, well coifed and wearing a wine-colored dress that undoubtedly cost more than I have in the bank. I imagine that Mrs. Duncan walking to the gas chamber will feel no more lost, no more a victim of what she's caught up in, than I do. I'm amazed by the back room. Instead of the cluttered storeroom I'd expected it looks more like a shrine. Strange. On one wall is a huge photograph of emaciated men staring through the fence of a Nazi death camp. The chilling reminder of what happened to millions of innocents makes me think again of Debbie's question: Is this the world? I read the plaque under the photograph and am stunned:

DO NOT FORGET

I ask for one thing of you who will survive this era: *do not forget*. Forget neither the good men nor the evil. Gather together patiently the testimonies about those who have fallen. One of these days the present will be the past, and people will speak of "the great evil" and of the nameless heroes who shaped history. I should like it to be known that there were no nameless heroes, that these were men who had names, faces, desires and hopes, and that therefore the suffering of even the least among them was no smaller than the suffering of the foremost whose name endures in memory. I wish that they may always remain close to you, like acquaintances, like kinsmen, like yourselves.

A CHRISTIAN CZECH RESISTANCE FIGHTER EXECUTED BY THE NAZIS

Staggered by the beauty and aptness of the words, I turn to face a moment I know I'll never forget. Torn between not being able to afford what Debbie wants and not wanting to disappoint her, I take refuge in my Southern childhood. There were no pet stores, but plenty of dogs for free unless you wanted a hound or a bird dog for hunting. While Debbie clicks toward the most expensive puppy in the store, I recall the starving dog I found in an alley, nearly hairless because someone had thrown scalding water on him. I begged Mother to let me keep the radiator-ribbed mongrel. Reluctantly, she agreed. The dog and I became inseparable.

Now, I realize that as much as I love my mother, something would have gone out of that love had she refused to let me keep the dog.

I bite my lower lip and make a vow: I might face a bookless future, but Debbie is not going to have a puppy-less present.

Vell says, "This is the only New Guinea Singing Dog in this country. It's a living relic of the stone age."

The price of the living relic surpasses what I paid for my car. Debbie's bound to be disappointed. The living relic yips at Debbie and she asks the owner, "Ma'am, may I hold him?" Vell nods, lifts the puppy out of its cage. The puppy squirms, licks Debbie's face as she laughs.

As she continues to play with the puppy, I wish I hadn't vowed to buy one for her.

Finally, she hands the puppy back to Vell. "May I see the other one, ma'am?"

The sickly looking mutt in the next enclosure is worse than puny. She almost falls down each time she wags her tail. No chance, puppy, I think, but Debbie beams, puts her nose against the glass. The puppy barks and limps toward the glass, licks it in greeting.

Even before Debbie speaks I know this is her puppy. The hair rises on my arms and I feel the needling rush I often feel when everything is right.

"Daddy may I have this one, please?" Her eyes fill with a pleading look.

I'll sell the car and walk or bicycle to work if I have to. "How much, ma'am?"

"Five hundred," Vell says with the insouciance of the very rich.

I've lost a book contract and I'm about to empty our checking account. I hand the gimpy animal to Debbie who giggles while the puppy squirms happily.

Vell whispers, "Five hundred pennies. I said five hundred because I want your daughter to think that the puppy is worth more. Now I see that nothing I could say would increase its value to her. They're perfect for each other."

Voice thick with gratitude, I thank Vell, pay her and say, "I know the puppy cost more than that. Why did you sell—"

Vell holds up her hand. "Your little girl's leg braces remind me of my sister, Anna, who died in Sobibor. Anna had polio so was among the first to go into the ovens."

Vell stops talking; her eyes pool. She swallows audibly, takes in a lung-filling breath. "The gentle way you care for your daughter reminds me of the way Papa cared for Anna."

Her voice breaks and her aristocratic face melts. She bites her lower lip. "I knew...knew when your daughter fell in love with that poor animal that this would be one of those rare instances when there would be profit in red ink."

It's then I notice the tell-tale number on her wrist. Should I say

I'm sorry for what she and her family suffered? No, that would serve no purpose. I decide to try to lighten things.

"Profit in red ink. Hmmm. In that case, how about that relic-of-the-stone-age puppy?"

Vell is still laughing when we leave the store, the puppy licking Debbie's face while her giggling blends with the sound of clicking braces and the puppy's happy yipping. In brisk wind seasoned with chimney smoke, aspen leaves flow by in golden flutters or flicker and whisper in the trees. I study Aspen's natural and man-made beauty, think of what Vell and other Jews suffered, think of Vell's kindness in spite of what she's endured, think of how good can triumph over evil, generosity over greed.

Yes, Debbie this...this is the world.

Mainstream/Literary Short Story Winner

STAINED

TERESA LITTLE
Jacksonville, FL

If you had told any of us that our sessions would bond us forever like sisters, we all would have thought you were the crazy one. One session a week, our faces changing, disappearing, reappearing, celebrated then lost forever until a crazy laugh, strangled cry or muddy cup of coffee, stale chocolate covered donut and cigarette ash converge to remind you; this was real. It is our story, fragmented, lost, hopeful and waiting to be told. Secrets yearn to be free.

It is perhaps why I am standing on the dirty concrete steps of a place I do not want to be. A small sign, black with one-inch white lettering gleams accusatorily in the fading twilight. It makes me think about secrets and lies piled one on top of another until I do not know where they began. Was I six, ten, fifteen or just born with the gift of the harmless white lie? Cannot quite call them harmless anymore, nor can I call them lies. My chest tightens and my stomach summersaults; the ritual has begun. I fish out two Rolaids between drags on my cigarette. Yummy, cherry flavored chalk.

"You going in now?" Mya glances briefly up at me then back at her shoes. She pulls her ratty black coat closer to her body as if it were a shield. Two sizes too big for her ample frame I bite my tongue to keep from proclaiming that she looks heavier. Content with her wardrobe she has rebuked my attempts to take her shopping. Although, underneath her frumpy clothes, mousy hair and fat, Mya has the potential for great beauty. With a simple makeover she could pass for pretty, no makeup needed, just a change of clothes, a haircut, hell, a comb. I again fight to maintain my tongue. We all have our mechanisms for protection. Looking bad is Mya's. It lends credence to my theory about God being cruel. In my quest to be beautiful I have waxed, bleached, Botoxed, and yes, altered body parts. Not to mention my daily ritual of makeup, lotion, and age defying creams. As the swell of my tantrum crests, I inhale most of my cigarette in one drawn out breath to keep from popping Mya on the back of the head. Mostly, I think I just want to alienate the one person willing to stand by me.

"In a minute." I say throwing the butt to the ground and grinding it against the step. My throat closes at the thought of another cigarette but I search for one anyway. I have discovered I will do anything to stall the inevitable. Kesi slinks to my side. She has the uncanny knack of showing up whenever a cigarette pack opens. Her hazel eyes dart from the Salem Lights in my hand to the faces of the surrounding smokers. Aware her cigarette pickings are slim she continues her approach.

"Hey." She gives a small nod. "Can ya spare one?" Kesi pats the pockets of her thin jersey jacket. "I'm out." Of course she is. "One cig." Kesi says sensing my reluctance. "Come on, Cate." She gives a megawatt smile that displays the impoverished soul incarcerated in her five-foot-two frame. All I see is a former junkie having replaced one addiction with another. Repulsed I relent. The smile on her face widens as she snatches the cigarette from my outstretched hand then falls faster than she can retreat. Kesi will have smoked half my pack before the end of the night.

Staring from Kesi to Mya beside me, I wonder how my life spiraled down to this. Mya shrugs, at what I'm not sure. "I don't really want to go in either." She says picking up our pre-Kesi conversation. The timbre of her voice breaks just a little at the end. Those puppy dog eyes of hers turn toward me. I want to claw them out. Yet, instead of following my predacious nature I find myself drawn into their pain. Deep brown pools trap me in a labyrinth similar to my own—with one difference. Mya accepts her burden, carries it in a way that makes her stronger. Despite her safe little life, the false starts, the forgotten and broken dreams, one thing remains certain. Mya will be free. It sits there hidden amongst the pain, the brief flicker of hope and a willingness to endure.

"I don't mind going in." I quip. "It is sitting in those damn plastic chairs. I feel like I am back in high school. Don't quite remember them being so uncomfortable." To emphasize my point I stretched my back.

"You haven't sat in a chair worth less than a hundred dollars in fifteen years. Why would you remember?" Pride widens her mouth into a smile that falters once her synapses catch their mistake. I am a fallen idol who let the pedestal explode beneath her feet. None guessed I would self-destruct, or that my incident with Ray would accelerate the process. After all I have slain courtroom monsters, heeled and tempered them to my bidding, invited a few to my bed, all to prove my dominance and take my rightful place as a partner at Williams, Cierce, and Danes. Yet here I stand on the front step of a government run "public assistance" agency wishing the lung cancer I'll get if I live to be sixty-three will take me now. My, my, how quickly the mighty fall and all without a sound.

The streetlight beside us clicks on. It's harsh light gleams off the black plastic of the sign causing the words to blur in a line of white then darken under the swaying shadow of a nearby tree. Suicide is the only legible word and I wonder if God is taunting me. Parts of me are so far gone I'd swear I did die and am shadowing Mya except the constant ache of an unsettled life remains. Death is a blissful thought unfulfilled. The one thing I crave yet can not seem to do. I'm now treated with kid gloves and marked fragile—do not shake. I could blame it on Ray, the sudden flashbacks, or the cocktails downed with a few pills but really it boils down to me. I am weak. Having made a career worthy of my prestigious law degree and climbed the socioeconomic ladder, I thought I had strength. Now I find it was just ambition. The consummate actress; I should have won an Oscar by now, maybe two.

"Time to go." Mya says eyeing a group of people solemnly plodding out. They are our queue to enter. Squaring my shoulders, I walk against the crowd exuding a fortitude I do not feel. This place stifles me. Here I am no longer the tigress strutting in my domain but a scared little girl. The beige décor and lime green floors meant to soothe have the opposite effect. Instead of the sense of hope, shelter and love I am meant to feel as I walk past the fake three-dollar ferns and poster board prints, anger and pain ooze from too many wounds to count. I long for the whirl of the fast lane and the freedom to plunge over the cliff. This little support group will not save me. There is nothing left to save. The demons ravished me long ago.

Fear rushes into the cracks of my façade. My steps slow. Kesi passes us in the hall. "See ya in there." As my smoking buddy she is obligated to give encouragement. I want to run and cannot. I'm trapped just like I was in the hallway of Stephen's building when Ray attacked me, just like I was twenty-seven years ago. Panic sets in; memories blur, his body over mine, breathing in the whisky fumes, counting in my head, just waiting for it to end, for him to pass out or roll away. I shiver involuntarily.

Mya grabs my hand. "He can't hurt you anymore." There is amazing strength in her grip; ferocity burns in her brown eyes. She thinks my fear stems from Stephen's neighbor, Ray. I wish it did. When Ray assaulted me, I beat the shit out of him. I pay dearly for that brief sense of empowerment. The demon long since buried unearthed itself the moment I smelled the whisky on Ray's breath. It has since refused to return to the grave.

"Bringing up the rear again?" It is Idona Sigrid, our therapist. Her short hair curls around her head in a silver cloud. A warm smile enlivens her wrinkles. The grandma disguise and sweet voice do not fool me. She is the wicked witch of any fable. A plump hand falls gently on my shoulder. My spine goes rigid. Idona assesses my body language. "Don't forget to breathe. Big breath in," her ample chest and diaphragm expand, "and out." She pats my shoulder. "Ready?" Mya pulls me forward before I can answer. Into the room then a plastic school chair I go.

My thigh trembles underneath my fingers, it is not noticeable except for the light scattering of ash pattering my jeans. We aren't supposed to smoke in the classrooms but Idona has been bending the rule. Lucky us. Anastasia is waving her hand in front of her face to keep the smoke away. It is attracted to the one nonsmoker in the room and encircles her completely. She interrupts her babble with a well-timed cough all of us including Idona ignore as she rambles on about her son. Anastasia could still be talking about Alaster or a sex scandal with the President of China; neither would hold my attention. All I can think about is the large bottle of vodka waiting for me at home. Maybe tonight I will find my strength and end this torture. I toy with the idea, aware the relief it brings is real.

"You gonna smoke that or let it burn out?" Kesi whispered in between Anastasia's crying jag. The forgotten cigarette burned slowly between my fingers. Licking her lips, Kesi leaned closer. "Cate?" She hated seeing anything go to waste especially something as precious as a cigarette. I know because she told me. I smile at my private joke. Here I am supposed to be listening to these women pour their hearts out and the one thing about the woman next to me that I remember is how she feels about cigarettes. I hand it to her. "Thanks."

"Okay Anastasia." The singsong voice with the ability to make my stomach crawl up and behind my heart says. "Thank you for sharing." Paper rustles as Idona flips to a clean sheet on her yellow legal pad. One more page and it will be my turn. "Berta, whenever you are ready." Idona's tone is softer, more commanding.

The plump Spanish woman beside me sits straighter in her seat. We wait silently as she runs a hand through her dark hair. I find it hard to believe we are here for the same reason considering her inch long salt and pepper roots. Berta glances up at the yellowed ceiling and mumbles a prayer. "You young ones," her black eyes float over Mya and Kesi, "you can learn from Anastasia and I." Kesi groans.

"You'll have your turn." Idona interrupts, "Go on Berta."

"You can not be victims forever. Nor can you stay angry. It will eat your soul away." I tuned out the minute she said victim. I am not a victim. Besides what could this old woman teach me? She is sobbing about her daughter Maria calling her granddaughter a slut for wearing a low cut dress and how it reminds her of what her own mother said after she learned Berta's cousin raped her. Television is more realistic than this. I want her to shut up but when she does it will be my turn. Leaning my head back and shutting my eyes, the irony does not elude me. God likes torturing people. He does it subtly by sending you a guardian angel, or two or three to mess with your head. Like the overzealous paramedic who refused to let me die. I figure that is how He keeps you from knowing which one will end up saving your ass.

Berta has stopped talking. I can hear her sniffles and ragged breath. She is done purging; my time begins. Sitting up, I am surprised by my calm. It fades quickly. Here come those cold grey eyes probing beneath an already raw exterior. My thigh bounces my hand on my leg. "Feel up to talking today, Cate?" Idona asks. Not really, I think to myself. I do not belong here with these losers sobbing out their guts for free. This is a mistake. A huge horrible mistake perpetrated by some lunatic judge I used to call my friend. I'm fine. My life is great. I have a six-figure salary, fancy car, and big house. One does not inherit these things; I earned them. Trapped in my throat my words are swimming in acid. Then it happens, I make the face and start gagging.

"Just like clockwork." It is Kesi talking yet I am already out of my seat and racing for the door. One day though, I might decide to stay seated and bathe her with my stomach contents. I have the beginning signs—I shake right before I vomit—but we all know I'll do anything to evade speaking. Last time I avoided it by excusing myself to the restroom. Idona informed me we went before or after session yet let me go since it was my second time at group. The first session was the best. She simply asked if I had anything to say. I shook my head no. Since then, no has become an inappropriate response. "I swear Doc, why do you bother? She ain't gonna talk. Hell, she couldn't talk her way out of a court appointed program. Must be some fine crackerjack law degree she has not to be able to do that!"

"Shut up!" Mya snapped. It was the last thing I heard as the door closed behind me. I knew Idona would moderate their fight as she had the previous week. She believed in airing out our feelings and my little ritual proved to be the ideal catalyst. It annoyed the group. Gone was the pity, the empathy of week one. I have managed to talk myself into feeling sick and continue gagging as I run towards the bathroom. The brain is a wonderful thing. Standing over the toilet spitting out random pools of saliva, I wait for the lining of my soul to bubble forth from my lips. The pain is unending. I'd swear I am hemorrhaging except no blood pollutes the water confined in the porcelain bowel. Torn in two, half of me a ball of rage that incinerates the flesh, the other, cold, lifeless as the Arctic. The cycle begins again. I am beyond vodka; the pain numbs itself. Temptation dances seductively before me and moves sweetly amongst my thoughts until the desire to end it all takes over. Who would ever know?

"You okay in there?" I let out a low groan. Mya, sweet, fat little Mya coming to rescue me. Her loyalty (once commendable and necessary as my personal secretary) annoys me now. If I had any energy I would slam her against the wall and watch her face turn from red to blue. I hate her and love her all within the same nanosecond.

"I'm fine." I say opening the stall door and heading to the sink to wash my hands. I must keep it together long enough to get home and find the bottle of sleeping pills stashed away in my suitcase. Thankfully, I never told anyone about them. Half a bottle of Smirnoff is buried under my winter sweats and the Absolute is hidden amongst the cleaners under the kitchen sink.

"I'm sorry about Kesi." Mya clears her throat. "She is just scared." Aren't we all? It hangs there in the air, the unsaid, the hurt, hers and mine. Does that make it ours? Lord knows our lives are more than intertwined. It is her story that echoes in the recesses of my brain when sleep evades me. Her sorrow, rages, and pain buried in layers beneath that plate of armor that she wears. I will never understand the intricacies of her soul. I barely understand my own. Still it lingers, pervading the air with its own breath. Fear. The dragon we all face.

"Forget about her." I stare at Mya through the mirror. She gives me a sad half nod. Her shoulders slump in defeat and her brown puppy dog eyes are downcast. She is again that petrified mouse I hired almost two years ago. I never thought she would last the day let alone a week.

Few secretaries lasted beyond their three-month evaluation. I demand an excellence that borders perfection. I did not claw my way up to the top on looks alone. Of course, it never hurt to sleep with a boss or two along the way. I had been young, ambitious. My eyes dart back to my reflection. What used to be beautiful is now old, tired and wretched. Dark circles line dull green eyes, stringy blond hair hangs limply against cheekbones that are too prevalent. My skin is pallid and flaky despite my weekly facial. Today I will blame it on the wonderful effects of alcohol. It certainly could not be work. A week ago my license was suspended. I am on "sick leave" at the firm. Nor could it be from a late night of entertaining since Stephen left me. Why be honest and admit to myself that I pushed the one man I ever loved away? Why put the blame on the person in the mirror? As together and strong as she looks, the truth would tumble her like a house of cards.

The scars on my wrists flare a dark red against my white skin. I wish they had let me finish the job. Lord knows I tried. If I had not of given Mya a house key, if she had arrived a few minutes later, if the paramedics got caught in traffic. They hadn't, nor would they of. Angels will not let you die regardless of how badly you want to. The proof is standing behind me. She is not much to look at, my angel. Rotund with gentle eyes and a skittish personality anyone would believe she is a pushover. I did. However, she is the survivor. For all my accolades I will never have that steel determination which keeps her sane and fighting. I envy that, for it was all I ever wanted. All I believed I had. She knows this too for she is already spouting the words I hate hearing. "Idona will make you come back." Doesn't she know it is too painful to listen to their stories? Their collective wounds tear away the vestiges of my defenses. I am nothing but a quivering body of goo. My secret, kept all these years is fighting to be free.

"I have nothing to say." *Keep quiet.* These two words crowd my brain in a loud crescendo that forces me to clinch my jaw. "I'm not ready."

"Sometimes we never are." Mya gives my hand a gentle squeeze. She leans against the counter. I felt it coming, the life altering speech that would save me. "All you can do is take it day by day moment by moment." I wrinkled my nose, sounded more like Hallmark. "Personally," Mya leaned closer whispering as though she were sharing a really dirty secret, "I'm not going to give the bastard the satisfaction of keeping me down." Her pupils dilated then narrowed to pinpricks, her mouth flattened in a grim line changing the demeanor of her face from prey to predator. I knew she was speaking of her father and the incest. "I'll see you in there?"

I gave a slight nod. Clarity for the first time in years loomed before me. Mya had given me the one key I overlooked. With a final glance at the mirror I left the safety of the restroom. The urge to rush straight for the double doors with the red neon exit sign beckoned. Instead, I turned left back down the hall towards the smoke filled classroom. As I neared the doorway I saw Mya speaking to the group. I did not need to hear her to know the horror she suffered as a child. We had talked about it a few times since I slit my wrists and once before then when we were both pretty drunk. I waited until she finished before opening the door.

"Feeling better?" Idona asked with one eyebrow raised. She slid the yellow paper backward to the skipped page I knew had my name written on it. Did she sense tonight was different?

"Yeah." I gave a weak smile as I took my seat in the circle. "I think I would like to say something." The room stills. I can hear the varied breaths of the women around me. Each waits; intent on listening to the words set to fall from my lips. It is a courtesy I never showed any of them. Kesi fidgets anxiously. Her hazel eyes are wide, curious. They give me the courage to continue. "My name is Catherine Saxsan. I am here because I have great friends" I chewed the inside of my bottom lip "and suicidal thoughts. Tonight after Mya checked in on me, I planned to down a bottle of sleeping pills and chase it with a bottle of vodka. Stupid, huh, telling you? Guess my fear of death is stronger than the pain." I pause. "I know you think it started with Ray." I was talking to Mya now. "I thought fending him off would make me feel better. Prove once and for all I can take care of myself." My voice started to tremble. "I've lost Stephen, jeopardized my career, my life and over what? A drunk getting too friendly?" The shroud of lies lifts and the truth takes to the air in my heavy sigh. "Ray was a catalyst." My chest constricts. "Little things surfaced, you know, snatches of childhood, dreams about my uncle. Thing is, they weren't dreams." My eyes searched the others then the secret burst free. "I was a victim of incest." Tears slide down my cheeks. Faces caught in momentary brilliance emerged, fractured yet pure. We cried. All except Idona, a small congratulatory smile announced my first step. The shadows over my heart receded displaying the vibrant colors of life. Like the stained glass windows in an old church, one does not truly appreciate their beauty without the sun. So it is with us.

Six women, all different, all in need. Each heart tainted, soiled and struggling through overlapping stages of cleansing. Each soul ravaged, damaged, sinking and fighting to maintain. Serenity wavers before our stinging eyes, taunting and always just beyond our grasp. Comfort hides in our similarities, our differences and solace in the tracks of our tears. Funny how we come together swearing no one understands our individual pain. Sitting in our safe circle I used to marvel at the collective lessons shared. Some found us, and others, we them. More await us still, hidden in the depths of the human psyche, in the rush of life's blood and the revolutions of earth. No moment lasts forever. As my mother used to say, you have to join the parade before it passes by. I get that now. The journey I have begun holds more lessons than I ever thought I could learn. Here amongst these women, I found my courage. Sitting vulnerable and raw, I found I am not as stained as I used to be.

Memoir/Personal Essay Winner

EDDIE

LORI LOSON
Littleton, CO

It's Friday, almost 4 o'clock, and I'm tired as I pull onto Cedarwood Drive, a narrow street behind the freeway densely lined with squalid apartment buildings. Uniformly dingy, there is little to distinguish one building from another as I drive slowly along the street searching for the address at the top of my referral sheet. *Eddie Perrone, 802 Cedarwood, Apartment 3.*

I recognize several children playing in a dusty patch of scrub grass and dirt in front of Building 802; students from the elementary school where I work. It's my job to assess "at risk" kids, and Cedarwood is one of the riskiest in the district. Several young faces gawk as I ease my car into a tight space between a battered pickup truck and a Dodge Dart with no front tires. I feel the stare of a disheveled man slouched on a concrete step across the street.

"Hey, Mrs. Loson!" This the unmistakable voice of a little blond spitfire named Blake, an irrepressible third grader who manages to get himself banished either to the Principal's office or mine on a regular basis. I'd last met with him a few weeks before at the insistence of his social studies teacher, who took offense when Blake produced a Picasso-like character with one eye and enormous breasts rather than a tracing of the African continent, as assigned. He grins at me now and offers to carry the file folder I tucked under my arm while locking the door of my car.

"You going to see Eddie?" he asks, his face a picture of earnest altruism. "I'll show you where he lives."

According to the scanty information I'd been given, Eddie Perrone was a five year old new to the neighborhood. I had yet to receive his medical reports and knew only that he had disabilities severe enough to prevent him from attending school. It was my job to make contact with the family, evaluate the situation, and recommend whatever special services the school district could provide for him.

Any case involving a seriously handicapped kid saddened me, but this one all the more so because of the obvious poverty that added to the family's burden. I'd long ago learned to keep an emotional distance from circumstances like this one that would otherwise either break my heart or inspire silent rage. It wasn't uncommon to find kids surviving situations here on Cedarwood that made me want to rant at their parents: *Why don't you clean yourself up, get a job, and take care of your children!*

36

Blake dashes across a cracked and pitched slab of concrete at the foot of a narrow stairway on the side of Building 802. I follow slowly, being careful not to step in the generous array of dog droppings that litter my path. I head up the stairway, a dim enclosure that smells vaguely of urine. Above me, Blake is pounding on the door, calling out, "Mr. Perrone, the lady from school is here!" Mr. Perrone, I note. *Another dad who doesn't work?*

The man who greets me at the top of the stairs smiles shyly, extends his hand, and says "Thank you for coming." He is maybe 30 years old, short, skinny, a noticeable gap in his smile where he is missing several teeth. His hair is carefully combed, his clothing clean, and—something I'd learned to size up quickly—he's sober.

"I'm Michael Perrone," he says, still shaking my hand. "Glad to meet you."

The front door opens directly into a bare living room, just like every other apartment I'd visited in this neighborhood, but there the similarities end. The room is neat and clean. A television tuned to *Sesame Street* plays softly. On the floor in front of the TV sits a well-padded infant seat, and in that seat, a child. Michael Perrone graciously offers me a cup of coffee and asks me to have a seat on a worn green sofa against the wall.

"My wife ain't home from work yet," he explains. "But me and Eddie's here!" I suppose my confusion shows on my face as I glance around the apartment. "That's Eddie there," he says, pointing toward the infant seat. I had yet to get a good look at the child, but had assumed it was a sleeping baby. Michael leaps from his chair and crouches on the floor near the child. "We got company, Bud," he croons, his voice as gentle and soft as lamb's wool. Slowly he turns the seat in my direction, and for the first time, I see the face of Eddie Perrone.

Five year olds go to Kindergarten. They climb jungle gyms and bring treasures to school for show and tell. They learn their ABCs and get in fights and insist on wearing only their favorite clothes. Eddie Perrone struggles to breathe. A plastic tube is attached through cotton batting and sterile tape to his delicately scarred neck. He couldn't weigh more than 20 pounds. At the sound of his father's voice, Eddie's fragile limbs tremble, his eyes widen, and his small mouth forms a smile. I swear to God, he smiled.

"You're a good boy, you're such a good boy," Michael Perrone sings. He looks up at me, genuine pride on his face. "They told us he wouldn't live to be five years old," he says. Looking back at the child, Michael reaches out a rough-skinned finger and gently strokes the boy's cheek. "You showed them, didn't you?" he whispers.

"Mr. Perrone, the district will have services to offer you," I say quietly.

"Aw, we don't need much of nothin'," he says. "We're doing just fine. I know Eddie won't never go to school and all."

In my folder there are forms and questionnaires that must be

37

completed. There are mountains of paperwork ahead, procedures to follow, agencies to contact. It will get done, but not now. I lay my folder aside and sit down on the floor next to Eddie. There is work to be done, but for now, I can only sit in reverent silence while Michael Perrone introduces me to his son.

Non-rhyming Poetry Winner

MY WOMAN

CHRISTO PRETORIUS
Pretoria, South Africa

My woman with her heart of secrets
With her heart a furnace refining my passions
My woman with her labyrinth thoughts
With her mind shining as the Badoura
My woman with her eyes of ice green fire
With her smile she lights a room of priests
My woman with her voice birthed in a crystal
With her voice she commands the mortals
With her charms she commands the gods
My woman with her lips parting like a ripe peach
With her oyster tongue of silk
And naked throat of nectar creme champagne
My woman with her hands as puppies ears
My woman with her shoulders of molten honey
With her dripping red plums
My woman with her gypsy hips
And her platinum crown
My woman with her dark, fragrant crown
My woman with the map of the universe on
the soles of her feet

Rhyming Poetry Winner

BACKWARDS THROUGH WET GRASS
for Anthony Hecht

ANNA EVANS
Hainesport, NJ

This Jersey fall, the unrelenting rain
has turned the front yards wild, their long, green hair
to otters' root-slick pelts. Today, again
I step out into gray, breathe loamy air
and catch a scent of home, a British field
I camped in once—a weekend trip to study
frogs. By day we kept our bodies sealed
in waterproofs, our feet twice-socked in muddy
boots. At night we hid in tents, played games
of "Crazy Eights" beneath the pitter-pat
of rain, now drumming our roll call of names,
now scrabbling on the canvas like a rat.
We were fourteen—all hormones—huddled damp
and close, a nest of rabbits, screened from sight
by tent flaps, while our teachers' hipflask camp
was pitched a hundred yards away. One night,
alone with me, Rob Murphy raised his hand
and touched my cheek. I shivered like a doe
for her first buck. He twined a loosened strand
of my dark hair around his thumb. I know
I twisted with it. He removed my glasses—
no one had ever done that—and he said
that I was pretty. Afterwards, in classes
I would stare at the back of his blond head
and dream of nameless acts. He nearly kissed
me, but our friends returned. The moment drained
away like runnels in the evening mist,
and came to nothing. Here, now it has rained
so much, that field, that clumsy, gentle boy
come back to me, and I remember this:
the thrumming rain, the unexpected joy
I knew at fourteen, for his almost-kiss.

Stage Play Winner

THE SEQUENCE
PAUL MULLIN
Seattle, WA

PLACE: Various

TIME: 1993-2001

CHARACTERS: Blue / Ruth   a woman, early 30s
              Green / Francis   a man, early 50s
              Red / Craig   a man, early 50s
              Yellow / Eleanor   a woman, late 50s

ACT I

Scene 1: *The "This is You" Fugue*

(Blue holds up a clear plastic bag filled with very long, thin strips of paper with seemingly random sequences of blue, yellow, green and red.)

BLUE
This is you.

GREEN
This is a blueprint for you.

RED
This is a semiotic representation of a blueprint for you.

YELLOW
This is a somewhat facetious, albeit intellectually accessible, semiotic representation of a blueprint for you.

BLUE
This is a genome.

RED
Everything you need to know to grow a human being is contained in this garbage bag, in a language of only four letters.

GREEN
It's too small.

RED
What?

GREEN
The bag's too small. You'd need a room full of bags that size to represent a human genome. It's got roughly three billion discrete letters.

BLUE
For the computer geeks in the audience, that's 750 megabytes of data.

YELLOW
For the more literary among us, that's a library of 5,000 books.

GREEN
For you kids, it's a single DVD. And in your life time don't be surprised to own one of these with your own personal genome burned onto it.

BLUE
You'll be able to take it with you to the emergency room when you break your ankle playing adult soccer 20 years from now.

GREEN
You'll be able to cross-reference potential mates.

YELLOW
Meow!

BLUE
Fully extended, the DNA of a single cell would stretch about six feet, but folded up it fits into a cell nucleus about half of a hundredth of a millimeter in diameter.

YELLOW
Go figure.

BLUE
To spell it out loud—

YELLOW (underneath)
G-G-T-G-G-C-G-C-G-A-G-C-T-T-C-T-G-A-A-A-C-T-A-G-G-C-G-
G-C-A-G-A-G-G-C-G-G-A-G-C-C-G-C-T-G-T-G-G-C-A-C-T-G-C-
T-G-C-G-C-C- G-G-T-G-G-C-G-C-G-A-G-C-T-T-C-T-G-A-A-A-C-
T-A-G-G-C-G-G-C-A-G-A-G-G-C-G-G-A-G-C-C-G-C-T-G-T-G-G-

C-A-C-T-G-C-T-G-C-G-C-C- G-G-T-G-G-C-G-C-G-A-G-C-T-T-C-T-G-A-A-A-C-T-A-G-G-C-G-G-C-A-G-A-G-G-C-G-G-A-G-C-C-G-C-T-G-T-G-G-C-A-C-T-G-C-T-G-C-G-C-C- G-G-T-G-G-C-G-C-G-A-G-C-T-T-C-T-G-A-A-A-C-T-A-G-G-C-G-G-C-A-G-A-G-G-C-G-G-A-G-C-C-G-C-T-G-T-G-G-C-A-C-T-G-C-T-G-C-G-C-C- G-G-T-G-G-C-G-C-G-A-G-C-T-T-C-T-G-A-A-A-C-T-A-G-G-C-G-G-C-A-G-A-G-G-C-G-G-A-G-C-C-G-C-T-G-T-G-G-C-A-C-T-G-C-T-G-C-G-C-C- G-G-T-G-G-C-G-C-G-A-G-C-T-T-C-T-G-A-A-A-C-T-A-G-G-C-G-G-C-A-G-A-G-G-C-G-G-A-G-C-C-G-C-T-G-T-G-G-C-A-C-T-G-C-T-G-C-G-C-C- G-G-T-G-G-C-G-C-G-A-G-C-T-T-C-T-G-A-A-A-C-T-A-G-G-C-G-G-C-A-G-A-G-G-C-G-G-A-G-C-C-G-C-T-G-T-G-G-C-A-C-T-G-C-T-G-C-G-C-C- G-G-T-G-G-C-G-C-G-A-G-C-T-T-C-T-G-A-A-A-C-T-A-G-G-C-G-G-C-A-G-A-G-G-C-G-G-A-G-C-C-G-C-T-G-T-G-G-C-A-C-T-G-C-T-G-C-G-C-C- G-G-T-G-G-C-G-C-G-A-G-C-T-T-C-T-G-A-A-A-C-T-A-G-G-C-G-G-C-A-G-A-G-G-C-G-G-A-G-C-C-G-C-T-G-T-G-G-C-A-C-T-G-C-T-G-C-G-C-C- G-G-T-G-G-C-G-C-G-A-G-C-T-T-C-T-G-A-A-A-C-T-A-G-G-C-G-G-C-A-G-A-G-G-C-G-G-A-G-C-C-G-C-T-G-T-G-G-C-A-C-T-G-C-T-G-C-G-C-C- G-G-T-G-G-C-G-C-G-A-G-C-T-T-C-T-G-A-A-A-C-T-A-G-G-C-G-G-C-A-G-A-G-G-C-G-G-A-G-C-C-G-C-T-G-T-G-G-C-A-C-T-G-C-T-G-C-. . .

BLUE

—Would take an entire lifetime.

GREEN

It takes a human cell about seven hours to faithfully copy an entire genome.

RED

95 percent of it is junk.

GREEN

What?

RED

Only five percent of the letters in your DNA actually transcribe into proteins that make up your body. The rest is just random—

GREEN

Well....

RED
—Meaningless stretches of letters. Junk.

GREEN
Maybe

RED
"Maybe?"

GREEN
Some say that 95 percent isn't junk at all, but maybe serves some purpose we don't know about.

RED
We're not really sure. There's a lot of stuff we're not sure about.

BLUE
In any case, imagine this room is filled with bags filled with strips like this. That's you.

GREEN
A blueprint for you.

RED
It's not a blueprint for you. Every one talks about blueprints. Forget about blueprints. A genome is really a lot more defiant of analogy than most people—even extremely educated people—like to think, but if it's like something, it's more like a recipe. Only...it's like a recipe...like a recipe... for...

YELLOW
Like a recipe for meatloaf written in hamburger!

BLUE
You are meatloaf written in hamburger.

GREEN
Man, that really takes the poetry out of it.

RED
Good. What's poetry got to do with it?

GREEN
Everything. The poetry of the recipe is the difference between life and nothing.

RED
The difference between you and me is a tenth of a percent.

BLUE
Red's right. No more than one in every thousand letters is different. In a bag like this, that's this much.

(Blue lets fall a sparse scattering of confetti.
Then points to Red and Green:)

These two, give or take two tenths of a percent, are you. And the same is true of any two of us.

YELLOW (to Blue)
But not the two of us.

BLUE
No. Right....Not us.

(indicating the bag)

This is you.

(indicating Green)

And this is you, give or take a percent tenth.

(indicating Red)

And so is this, to the same degree.
But this...

(Blue indicates Yellow, who ties a scarf around her own head, and then lays back in a special "chemo recliner," plugging an IV into her arm.

This is half of me exactly.
And she's dead.

ELEANOR
Let's say dying.

RUTH
This is my head.

ELEANOR
For the sake of the story.

RUTH
For Ma, everything's the story.

ELEANOR
Stories within stories within stories. Ad infinitum.

RUTH
Ad nauseum. You'll need to forgive her, she's a little doped up right now.

ELEANOR
Indulge me.

RUTH
When don't I ever?

ELEANOR
Tell it.

RUTH
Fine. The story...began...well...that's always a tough question, isn't it?... Depending on how you wanted to tell it, you could either say it began around 3.5 billion years ago when a certain sort of molecule began to arrange itself in such away that it could copy itself to arrange itself in a certain way that it could copy itself, ad infinitum—

ELEANOR
—Ad nauseum—

RUTH
Or you could say that the story began a little less than a decade ago, when my editor sent me to cover a reception in honor of the newly appointed head of the National Center for Human Genome Research.

Scene 2: *TIGR's Tale*

(Lights up on Francis speaking at a podium. Even though he's clearly in his best jacket and tie, he still has a rumpled slept-in look, which, along with his five-dollar hair cut, is almost enough to make one wonder if he hasn't purposefully cultivated his bumpkin image.)

FRANCIS
In 1987, my esteemed predecessor went before Congress to ask for an initial annual budget of 30 million dollars in order to begin an undertaking projected to ultimately cost some three billion dollars and not be finished until the year 2005, 18 years later. My esteemed predecessor had guts!

Now first, let me just say, if someone had told me as an undergraduate at UVA that I would be succeeding James Watson...I think I'd've probably told that someone to go toss himself in Lake Monticello. But... here I am. And here I face the greatest challenge of my life and face it gladly, proudly. For the work that was began by Dr. Watson will not be left undone.

Now let's try and get a little perspective. We're not talking about going to the moon here or splitting the atom. Our goal is something really important. But seriously, decoding the human genome, in terms of its implications for ourselves, carries even greater implications—medically, philosophically, and societally—than any previous organized scientific effort.

So, allow me to get down to brass tacks...

(Focus shifts from Francis to Ruth taking notes. Craig enters, dressed in a very sharp, very expensive suit. He watches along side Ruth for a moment, then turns and whispers to her:)

CRAIG
Looks like they picked the right guy to replace Watson.

FRANCIS (underneath)
Although the goal of sequencing DNA at a cost of 50¢ a base pair may be met by 1996, the rate at which DNA can be sequenced will not be sufficient for sequencing the whole genome. Priority should be given during the next five years to increasing sequencing capacity. Substantial new technology that will allow sequencing at higher rates and lower costs is also needed. These developments will only occur if significantly greater financial resources can be invested in this area. It is estimated that an immediate investment of $100 million per year will be needed for sequencing technology alone, to allow the human genome to be sequenced by the year 2005.

RUTH
You think so?

CRAIG
Oh, yeah. A very nice, safe choice, don't ya think?

RUTH
I don't know. I guess I'd be more interested in what you think and why, Mr.—

(looking at his badge)

Excuse me, *Doctor* Venter, of T.I.G.R.

CRAIG
The Institute of Genomic Research. We just call it "Tiger."

RUTH
Oooh. "Tiger."

CRAIG
And you work for?

RUTH
The Sun.

CRAIG
(handing her a card)
When you get bored covering the public sector dinosaurs let me know.

(Craig walks off. Focus draws back to Francis.)

FRANCIS
And as crucial as the Apollo and Manhattan projects were to the advancement of human knowledge, what could possibly be more important than reading the story of us written by the Almighty himself?

(Lights up on Eleanor cutting stir fry veggies.)

ELEANOR
Oh, so this one's gonna invoke the Almighty now? What, please tell me, ever happened to the good old-fashioned atheistic scientist?

(Ruth crosses and joins in the chopping.)

RUTH
I thought it was interesting he mentioned the Manhattan Project.

ELEANOR
Interesting how? Everyone in Big Science mentions the Manhattan Project as often as they can, like thumpers calling on an angry God.

RUTH
I meant it was interesting 'cause this is my first shot at an ongoing science story and you won your Pulitzer for your book on the Manhattan Project... and all.

ELEANOR
If it's the Pulitzer you want, you can have mine. It's in a frame I think somewhere... in the mud room, maybe.

RUTH
I don't want yours. I want my own.

ELEANOR
I didn't get mine by playing coquette with my subjects, that I can assure you.

RUTH
And what would make you say something as fucked up as that?

ELEANOR
It's my bitch gene. Must've skipped you. Maybe your friend can sequence it and fix me.

(Lights shift to Ruth interviewing Francis.)

RUTH
So, bottom line first: who cares? Why do we even need to sequence the human genome?

FRANCIS
Because a complete sequence compared to what we have now is like the difference between a high-def Landsat projection and one of those medieval maps that trails off at the edges with "Here be monsters." The better the map, the better we can cure diseases. That's the first answer. The rational grown-up answer. The second answer is: because it's there... just sitting there waiting to be known. We have what it takes to do it, so why not start? They're gonna be talking about this in 500 years the same way we talk about Cortez and Columbus.

RUTH
Some people nowadays have some pretty not nice things to say about Cortez and Columbus.

FRANCIS
Yes. That's true, too.

RUTH
In your speech, you mentioned the Almighty. I understand you're a born-again Christian. Can you talk a little bit about your faith and how it might come into conflict with a purely scientific mission such as this?

FRANCIS
Bit of a leading question, isn't it? But that's okay. I understand. There are a lot of people who balk at the notion of a scientist having a strong faith. The funny thing is: you could easily say I came to it through science.

RUTH
Really? How so?

FRANCIS
When I got out of high school I wanted to be a chemist. Biology held no interest for me at all. Somehow, I had the notion that life was chaotic, its governing principles unpredictable. But for my Ph.D. at Yale, I had to take biochem. It was only then I learned this amazing code that translates into life and I was completely blown away. This was the opposite of chaos. This was the language of divinity. Some years later, right around when I was graduating med school I became a Christian in the fullest sense.

When you think about it, what is science but the act of appreciating something that up until the moment it's discovered, no human has known, but God knew it? In a way, perhaps, these moments of discovery—and I've been lucky enough to have a few of them—also become moments of worship.

RUTH
How do you reconcile your faith with the knowledge that even today rudimentary prenatal genetic screening routinely leads to abortions?

FRANCIS
Yeah. Okay. Can we go off the record for a moment?

RUTH
Uh...sure.

FRANCIS
As a Christian, as a human being, I am troubled by abortion. As a doctor and a scientist I have an ethical obligation to keep these feelings to myself when consulting with a patient or a research colleague. But revving the issue, in a public way, in a newspaper interview for instance, only makes my job as a scientist and a physician harder. Okay?

RUTH
Okay...So on the record?

FRANCIS
On the record...whenever I or colleagues of mine get a little too sanguine about the benefits of genetics, I think of Woody Guthrie.

RUTH
The folk singer.

FRANCIS
That's right. And songwriter. I play guitar. And he's a bit of a hero for me. See Woody had Huntington's Disease. Huntington's is one of those few diseases that genetics can predict with absolute certainty. We can look at your fourth chromosome, even in utero, and if at a certain locus on Chromosome 4, you have this particular repetition of three letters, C-A-G, more than say 35 times, you'll become symptomatic for Huntington's some time in your 30s or 40s. And some ten to 15 years later, after a terrible, degenerative, debilitating process of brain cell necrosis, you'll die. No if, ands, or buts. And that's what happened to the guy who gave us, "This Land is Your Land." Genetic pathology is rarely clear-cut, but when it is, it can be merciless. And it leaves us with a kind of brutal question: once you begin to know a little bit what God knows, do you act on that limited knowledge? Do you abort Woody Guthrie?

There are so many issues here. Certainly, we need to take some of the resources we're spending to explore the genome and invest them in these moral questions.

RUTH
Speaking of moral issues, how do you feel about gene patenting?

FRANCIS
I see both sides of the argument. But I do think there are those in the private sector that look at the genome like conquistadors dreaming of El Dorado.

RUTH
Like who?

FRANCIS
Oh, I'm not going to get into naming names.

(Lights up on Craig.)

CRAIG
He means me.

RUTH
Like TIGR?

Scene 3: *Patent Nonsense*

FRANCIS
I'm really not interested in talking about specifics.

RUTH
Like TIGR?

CRAIG
Like me.

(Lights out on Craig.)

RUTH
How do you feel about Craig Venter?

FRANCIS
I have no feelings at all. I barely know the guy.

(Lights shift from Francis to Eleanor.)

ELEANOR
Interesting. You caught that, I hope.

RUTH
Yeah, he's bluffing.

ELEANOR
So?

RUTH
So if he's bluffing, he's hiding something.

ELEANOR
So?

RUTH
So, there's something there. A story maybe.

ELEANOR
A story maybe. So?

RUTH
So? I gotta call this guy at TIGR.

(She pulls out the card Craig gave her.)

Venter. Craig Venter.

ELEANOR
Catch a tiger by its toe.

(Lights shift to Ruth and Craig.)

RUTH
Some interviews are like pulling teeth. But this guy was spitting 'em at me.

CRAIG
You wanna know about gene patenting? I invented gene patenting. For better or worse, that was me. Reason number one the public sector chumps hate me. I inspired the invective of no less a giant in the field than James Watson, co-discoverer of the structure of DNA. Yeah. Guy sits in front of the Senate committee and tells 'em my methods aren't science, that what I do could be done by monkeys. Here I am, relatively young, relatively new to the field, and the Father of Genomics is busting my balls in front of the most powerful legislative body on earth. Nice. But hey! —trial by fire. Take what you get, right? I don't hold grudges. I'm not a vindictive person. I internalize anger and convert it into constructive energy.
And ultimately, on that score, I'm vindicated, cuz the Director of NIH backed me up and tossed the grand old man out on his ass, then brought in your eminently mild-mannered friend Francis Collins to replace him.

RUTH
What was the method Watson was criticizing?

CRAIG
Automated gene sequencing. Express sequence tagging. The future, basically—that's all—of genomic research.

RUTH
Express sequence—

CRAIG
Tagging. E.S.T. Look, only 3 to 5 percent of the genome actually encodes for genes, right? The rest is junk. So why go driving through the Mojave desert looking for an Arby's, right? In any given tissue sample there's gonna be RNA doing its stuff, transcribing into proteins. Right. So I suck up this RNA, dose it with some reverse transcriptase to lock it down into cDNA and boom! I got an E.S.T.

RUTH
Uh-huh.
He was going too fast. I needed to bone up on some basics just to understand what he was talking about.

(Lights up Eleanor.)

ELEANOR
You should've done your research.

RUTH
Fine!

(Lights shift.)

Scene 4: *Transcription Tango*

(Ruth becomes Blue, and pulls a long strip from one of the clear plastic bags.)

BLUE
This is a gene.

(She tears off a single colored bit.)

This is a base.

GREEN
One letter of DNA.

RED
There are four letters in all.

BLUE
A.

GREEN
C.

YELLOW
T.

RED
G.

54

GREEN
Though they're not actually letters.

RED
Of course not. They're molecules. But they act like letters.

YELLOW
What do letters act like?

BLUE
They spell things.

YELLOW
Letters don't spell things, people do.

BLUE
Cute. But bear with me—

(displaying a piece of confetti on her fingertip)

This is you.

RED
Divided by 3 billion.

BLUE
Each letter has a partner that it always matches up with.

BLUE & YELLOW
(simultaneously)
A to T.

GREEN & RED
(simultaneously)
G to C.

BLUE
These are base pairs.

GREEN
If the genome were the equator, a gene would be the size of a football field, and a base pair, a tiny pebble.

(Blue unspools a very long strip.)

BLUE
This is a gene.

YELLOW
Genes make proteins.

GREEN
Proteins make things alive. They are literally the building blocks and engine parts of life. Whatever needs doing in your body, proteins do it. And genes make 'em.

YELLOW
Yeah, but how?

BLUE
They spell 'em.

RED
Yeah, but how?

BLUE
The letters of DNA sequence copy themselves to RNA.

YELLOW
Yeah, but—

GREEN
Look, RNA's like DNA only it's not as long and not as permanent.

BLUE
And the "T" for thymine becomes a "U" for uracil.

RED
How come?

BLUE
Just cuz, 'kay?

RED
'Kay.

GREEN
So the DNA unzips.

(He tears a strip perfectly in half, lengthwise.)

                    BLUE
And the RNA copies it simply by matching up.

(RNA transcription is illustrated in some clever, theatrical but eminently accessible way, ala designer Gary Smoot. Maybe tinker toys or colored magnets; something very "Bill Nye, the Science Guy.")

                BLUE & YELLOW
                  (simultaneously)
T to A.

                 GREEN & RED
                  (simultaneously)
C to G.

                    GREEN
Now you have a nice portable strip of genetic code that you can take to a ribosome and translate into a protein.

                    RED
A ribo-who now?

                    GREEN
Ribosome! It's like a machine for making proteins.

                    RED
Oh.

                    GREEN
All you gotta do is feed one the RNA instructions on one side and they start building the protein on the other.

              (Again, see stage direction above.)

                    YELLOW
Yeah, but how?

                    BLUE
Spelling, remember.

                    YELLOW
Not really.

                    BLUE
Every combination of three letters of RNA, like—

57

GREEN
G-A-C.

RED
Gack!

GREEN
Or G-A-G.

YELLOW
Gag!

GREEN
Or U-A U.

RED
Oooaaaooo!

BLUE
Is called a codon.

YELLOW
Okay.

BLUE
And each codon matches up to either an amino acid or a punctuation mark.

YELLOW
A punctuation mark?

BLUE
Yeah. For instance.

GREEN
A-U-G.

RED
"aug!"

BLUE
Means

GREEN
"Start building a chain."

BLUE
So does G-U-G.

RED
"Gug!"

BLUE
Now, U-A-G, U-G-A, and U-A-A—

RED
"Ooag!, oooga!, aaa-aaa!"

BLUE
Mean—

GREEN
"Stop building the chain."

BLUE
Now. Say you want to start building your chain and you want to add an aspartate molecule.

YELLOW
Okay.

GREEN
Just spell G-A-C—

RED
Gack!

YELLOW
Uh... Okay.

GREEN
Or G-A-G—

RED
Gag!

BLUE
To add a glutamate.

GREEN
Or U-A U—

RED

Oooaaaooo!

BLUE

Tyrosine. And so it goes, working down the line of letters, three letters at a time, adding an amino acid like beads on a necklace until you reach.

RED

Ooag! Ooga! Or aaa-aaa!

GREEN

"Stop building the chain!"

(MORE)

Television/Movie Script Winner

OFF THE FOB

CATHERINE ROSS
Puyallup, WA

A BLACK SCREEN:

Heavy BREATHING and FOOTSTEPS of several can be heard.

FADE IN:

EXT. AHMED'S HOUSE—NIGHT

A doorway comes into green and black focus through NVGs (Night Vision Goggles). SPECIALIST HUXLEY and SPECIALIST HOOPER stack on one side of the doorway while SERGEANT JOHNNY BILLINGS crouches on the other side.

SUPER: "MOSUL, IRAQ, 2004"

The soldiers wear desert camo uniforms and full battle rattle—interceptor vests with ammo and radios attached, headsets on under Kevlar helmets with NVGs mounted, M-4 carbines at the ready. Huxley has a breach kit on his back.

A fourth soldier, Staff Sergeant ZANE BLACK, walks up to the door. He is tall and powerfully built with chiseled features and a serious countenance. He KNOCKS loudly. No response. He presses his ear up against the door to listen.

INT. AHMED'S HOUSE—SAME

AHMED, an Iraqi man wearing shorts and a wife-beater, peeks out of a window and sees the soldiers at his front door. He backs away from the window. His wife, IKROM, clings to his arm.

                    IKROM
        Why are they here? What did you do?

                    AHMED
        I don't know, I didn't do anything! Go upstairs with the

children. I'll be right there.

Ikrom leaves. Ahmed goes over to his couch and pulls out an AK-47 from behind it, then moves towards the stairs.

EXT. AHMED'S HOUSE—SAME

Zane signals to the other soldiers and they get to work putting C-4 on the door and connecting detonation cord. They walk the det cord out a little ways, crouch down, cover their ears, and let her blow.

BOOM!

The four soldiers flip their NVGs up and the screen goes from black and green to full color. They move rapidly towards the doorway.

INT. AHMED'S HOUSE—NIGHT

The four soldiers enter the house, weapons up, scanning. The living room is empty. Ahmed can just be seen running left past a doorway on the far side of the room.

Zane signals to Johnny to stick with him, and to Huxley and Hooper to clear the hallway going right.

Huxley and Hooper move out, then Zane and Johnny go left down the hallway. They make their way silently up a staircase.

At the head of the stairs is a closed door. Zane listens at the door. Hurried movements and whispering in Arabic can be heard. A magazine is being loaded into a rifle and a round is chambered.

Zane pulls a flash-bang grenade from his vest and holds it up for Johnny to see, who nods and plasters himself to the wall next to the door.

Zane pauses a split second, then kicks the door in, tosses the grenade, then plasters himself against the wall next to the door opposite Johnny.

There is a flash of light and a BANG! as the grenade explodes, followed by YELLING in Arabic. Smoke seeps out of the room. Ahmed struggles out of the room holding an AK-47. Zane slams him down on the ground and grabs the AK.

Johnny holds Ahmed down while Zane clears the AK and gets on the radio.

                    ZANE
    Three-Bravo, Blue-Three.

                SOLDIER ONE (V.O.)
                  (through static)
            Blue-Three, Three-Bravo.

                    ZANE
    Get the terp up here.

                SOLDIER ONE (V.O.)
    Roger.

Zane peers into the room. Ikrom crouches together with three frightened CHILDREN. Huxley searches Ahmed. He finds a wallet and pulls out an ID, which he hands to Zane.

SAM, the interpreter, shows up. Sam is a twenty-something Iraqi in civilian clothes, interceptor vest and black ski mask covering his face. Zane hands the ID to Sam who yanks up his ski mask and examines the ID.
                    SAM
        Ahmed Younis Yahya. 33 years old.

Zane looks at his notebook.

                    ZANE
    Goddammit!

Zane puts his notebook away.

                    ZANE
    Who the fuck sent us to this house?!

                    JOHNNY
    I triple checked the grid. It matches the imagery.

                    ZANE
    This is the second empty hole tonight. Can you tell me where the fuck this so-called intelligence is coming from?

Johnny raises an eyebrow and shrugs. Zane takes a deep breath.

                    ZANE
    Round up the family and take pictures of the damage. Bravo Team will finish the search.

                    JOHNNY
          Roger.

                    ZANE
                (into radio)
          Three-Bravo, Blue-Three.

                    SOLDIER ONE (V.O.)
          Three-Bravo.

                    ZANE
          Finish the search. I've got one AK up here. If you don't find
          anything else, we'll move out.

                    SOLDIER ONE (V.O.)
          Understood. Wilco.

                    ZANE
          Blue-Three out.

Keeping his eye on the family, Zane turns to Sam.

                    ZANE
          Tell them someone gave us bad information, because maybe
          someone doesn't like them. But we were told that this was
          the house of a bad guy. Tell them they can come to the FOB
          for damage compensation.

Sam nods and starts speaking in Arabic to Ahmed and his family.

EXT. UPPER CLASS IRAQI HOME—NIGHT

Zane and Johnny stand on the sides of a doorway.

                    ZANE
                (whisper)
          Last chance to get some tonight.

                    JOHNNY
          Then this is their lucky fucking day.

Zane kicks in the door with a yell and hurls himself inside.

INT. UPPER CLASS IRAQI HOME—NIGHT

The door swings open and crashes against the wall. Zane and Johnny
enter a high-ceilinged foyer, and Hooper and Huxley follow behind.

Light from a chandelier reflects off of the polished marble of the floors and pillars.

Hooper and Huxley start searching downstairs as Zane and Johnny go upstairs. They find an empty hallway with several closed doors.

Zane kicks in the first door and enters a large bathroom, Johnny following behind. They both aim their rifles at a well-groomed Iraqi wearing pajamas, ALI, crouched in the far corner, shakily cradling an AK-47.

Zane breathes hard and keeps his weapon trained on Ali. Johnny covers Zane.

                      ALI
    Fuck you, Americans!

Zane walks over to Ali, grabs the AK and yanks Ali to his feet.

                      ALI
    President Bush is donkey!

Zane shoves Ali in Johnny's direction.

                      ZANE
    Search him.

Johnny pats Ali down while Zane paces around the bathroom. He tears the shower curtain down off of the shower, then kicks the sink, which starts to come off the wall. He grabs it with his hands and rips it off the wall.

                      ALI
    Why! Why you do this!

                      ZANE
    You disrespect me, I disrespect you.

Johnny pulls a wallet out of Ali's pocket and finds an ID, which he hands over to Zane. Zane looks at the ID, which is old and beat up while Johnny yanks Ali's arms down and pulls his hands through flexi-cuffs, tightening them.

                      ZANE
    I got this. Go grab Sam.

Zane holds the ID up to Ali's face.

                      ZANE
    What kind of ID is this?

                    ALI
        Baath Party. I was leader in Baath Party.

Johnny and Sam walk in.
                    ZANE
        So you were loyal to Saddam?

                    ALI
        I still loyal to Saddam. I hate you. I hate Americans!

Zane hits Ali hard on the side of the head. Ali crumples to the ground. Zane hands the IDs over to Sam who studies them.

                    SAM
        Ali Mahmood al-Jafaari.

                    ZANE
             (checking his notebook)
        He's a match. At least we got one tonight.

                    JOHNNY
        You gotta see what the boys found in the backyard.

Zane and Johnny move toward the door, shoving Ali along in front of them.
                    ZANE
Oh?
                    JOHNNY
You'll like it.
                    ZANE
        Better be something I can blow up.

                    JOHNNY
        I'm sure you'll find a way.

EXT. UPPER CLASS IRAQI HOME—NIGHT

Hooper and Huxley stand on a mound of dirt with their backs to Zane and Johnny who walk toward them with Ali in hand and Sam following.

A tarp sits crumpled off to the side and Hooper is shining the tac light on his rifle down at the ground. Zane, Johnny, Ali and Sam join Hooper and Huxley and look down.

A large collection of AK-47s, 7.62 mm rounds, RPGs, mortars of various sizes, miscellaneous wires and electronics sit in a depression, partially covered with dirt.

> ZANE
> Parting gifts from the Baath Party?

Ali turns towards Zane as much as he can with a look of hate.

> ALI
> Fuck you! Fuck Americans! I kill many—

Zane lets go of Ali's arm and punches him square in the face. Ali doubles over and staggers, then regains his balance. Zane looks over at Johnny.

> ZANE
> Get this guy on a Stryker before I shitcan him beyond recognition. He's trying my fucking nerves.

> JOHNNY
> I'll take care of him. Should I send some guys back—

> ZANE
> Yeah, we'll need to load some of this crap up.

> HOOPER
> Hey sergeant, you want me to request EOD to come out here and dispose of the mortar rounds?

> ZANE
> Negative. I know I taught you better than that. We'll be here all goddamn night and day if we call them. I'll deal with it. Huxley!

Huxley walks up.

> HUXLEY
> Yes, sergeant.

> ZANE
> Give me your breach kit. You and Hooper clear this area and let me do my thing.

> HUXLEY
> Yes, sergeant.

Huxley hands his breach kit to Zane while giving Johnny a doubtful look. Johnny shakes his head slightly and pushes Ali in the direction of the street. Zane sets the breach kit down and opens it up.

EXT. UPPER CLASS RESIDENTIAL STREET—NIGHT

Johnny pushes Ali up the ramp and into a Stryker. Johnny hops in and walks to the front to a pair of legs belonging to SERGEANT FIRST CLASS FRANK. The rest of Sergeant Frank is in the hatch.

Johnny tugs on Sergeant Frank's pant leg. Sergeant Frank ducks down into the Stryker.

       JOHNNY
  He's at it again.

      SERGEANT FRANK
  Sergeant Black?

       JOHNNY
  Yes, sergeant. Friggin' suicidal.

Sergeant Frank sighs.

       JOHNNY
  Should I stop him?

      SERGEANT FRANK
  I know I should say yes, but no, don't stop him. As high as the shit's been stacked against him, he's always an excellent demo man.

EXT. UPPER CLASS IRAQI HOME—NIGHT

Hooper walks off with the last of the AKs and Huxley carries a box of wires and electronics components. Zane is down in the depression, carefully winding detonation cord around mortar rounds.

      JOHNNY (V.O.)
  Hasn't blown himself up yet, sergeant, but every time, I think he gets closer to doing it.

Zane finishes with the mortar rounds and leaves a tail of det cord to which he attaches the shock tube. He extends the shock tube out, going over and behind the dirt mound. To the end of this he attaches an M81 initiator.

Zane scans the area quickly, then pulls the initiator.

EXT. FOB (FORWARD OPERATING BASE) MAIN GATE—MORNING

BOOM!

A mortar round hits the temporary helicopter pad made of metal plates, tearing through the plates and sending shrapnel across the pad.

SERGEANT KILEY RAWLINGS, a young and pretty woman with a no-nonsense expression on her makeup-less face, crouches down on the road next to the helicopter pad leading to the main gate. She takes in a deep breath, then runs towards the gate.

Kiley makes it to one of several concrete barriers lined up in front of the small reception building by the gate and ducks down behind it when—

BOOM!

Another mortar round hits, this time impacting the road where Kiley had just run from. Shrapnel and small chunks of asphalt hit the barrier where Kiley crouches.

Kiley glances up and sees a GATE GUARD, a male soldier in full battle-rattle, crouched as she is behind the next barrier over. He points at the reception building. Kiley nods, and makes a run for the reception building.

INT. MAIN GATE RECEPTION BUILDING—MORNING

Kiley bursts through the door and lays flat on the floor, face to face with a frightened Iraqi man, LAITH, dressed in a traditional white "dress" (dish dasha) with matching white headdress.

BOOM! BOOM! BOOM!

Three more mortar rounds impact outside, sending showers of debris and shrapnel through the air and rattling the windows of the reception building.

Kiley stays on the floor, holding her breath. She looks around the small room equipped with a couch and television set. The floor is covered with frightened Iraqi civilians.

Finally, Kiley stands up and brushes off her uniform and glances down at the pistol strapped to her hip. She pulls a notebook and pen out of her cargo pocket and points at Laith, who stands up.

                        KILEY
               (motioning with her hand)
      Come with me.

Kiley walks to the back of the room and through a doorway into the CONFERENCE ROOM.

Kiley motions towards a long table with chairs and Laith takes a seat as Kiley closes the door. Kiley takes a seat across the table from Laith. She and Laith speak in Arabic the entire time.

                         KILEY
             What can I help you with?

Laith pulls out a stack of photos and hands them to Kiley. Kiley examines the pictures, which are of Ali's house following Zane's raid. Laith points angrily at some of the photos.

                         LAITH
             They ruined my door! And look at the sink!

Laith shows Kiley photos of the sink Zane ripped off the wall.

                         LAITH
             There is no reason for this! I am not a bad man. Soldiers say if I come here, you will pay for the damage.

                         KILEY
             Well, sir, I will verify this damage with the soldiers who came to your home. Come back tomorrow, and I can let you know the outcome.

                         LAITH
             Yes, yes. Thank you very much.

                         KILEY
             Can I hold onto these photos for now?

                         LAITH
             Yes, yes. Please.

                         KILEY
             Okay then. Good-bye.

Kiley stands and holds out her hand. Laith shakes it.

                         LAITH
             Good-bye.

Laith exits and a HUSBAND and WIFE enter. They both start talking at once, gesturing at each other. Kiley takes a deep breath and gets her pen and paper ready.

INT. AHMED'S HOUSE—DAY

Ahmed sits at his kitchen table with HUSSEIN, a chubby man with a five o'clock shadow and messy clothes. They sip quietly on little glasses of chai. They speak in Arabic.

      HUSSEIN
I can help you.

      AHMED
How?

      HUSSEIN
I can show you how to do things. I can introduce you to people. Me and my men, we can get things done.

      AHMED
I want him to be afraid. I want him to feel the pain I felt. My home violated. My wife, my children afraid. And there was no need.

      HUSSEIN
You are a smart man. Smarter than me. You just need to think in the right direction.

      AHMED
This American, this Sergeant Black, he won't know what hit him.

INT. CHOW HALL—DAY

Zane sits at a table with SERGEANT MAJOR NUTRO—a large man who looks intimidating, but has a big grin and easy laugh. He speaks with a slight southern accent. Both he and Zane eat sandwiches.

      SERGEANT MAJOR
I heard you had another near brush with suicide last night.

      ZANE
Yeah, didn't work.

      SERGEANT MAJOR
Zane, I'm not a mental health counselor, but I've been around, so we'll say I've got some wisdom to pass on. Are you ready?

ZANE
Not really.

SERGEANT MAJOR
You have more reasons to live than to die. You were the best that Delta ever had.

ZANE
WAS the best.

SERGEANT MAJOR
Well, I think you're man enough to admit that you're not in top form right now. I don't mean physically. I'm talking about your head.

ZANE
Sergeant Major, what happened in Afghanistan—

SERGEANT MAJOR
I know what happened, Zane. I know you saved a lot of lives. You were a hero.

ZANE
I wouldn't go that far. But it doesn't matter. Afghanistan was the worst thing that ever happened to me.

Kiley appears at their table.

KILEY
Sergeant Major, I'm sorry to interrupt but I need to check something with Sergeant Black.

SERGEANT MAJOR
Not a problem sergeant.

Kiley nods towards Sergeant Major, then looks at Zane.

KILEY
Sergeant, you led the raids last night?

ZANE
Yes, that was me.

KILEY
I've been dealing with damage claims all morning resulting from those raids.

ZANE
All morning. Wow.

KILEY
Was all the damage worth it? Did you find any bad guys?

ZANE
Found one.

KILEY
Sergeant, you realize you caused at least five thousand dollars worth of damage last night, possibly more if it turns out that that one bad guy is not a bad guy.

ZANE
I don't pick the houses. Some POG in the TOC does that. I'm given a target and I execute. That's how it works. Not my fault the intel sucks.

KILEY
Was it really necessary to rip the sink off the wall of the house in Al Hadba?

ZANE
Al what?

Sergeant Major is holding his head like it hurts.

KILEY
Al Hadba. The last neighborhood that you were in last night. Why do that to the sink? I don't understand.

ZANE
Sergeant, look. If I'm told to do a thorough search for a weapons cache, I'm gonna do a thorough search.

KILEY
Well, the owner of that home came to me this morning wanting us to pay for his sink and whatever else.

ZANE
That's impossible. The owner is in the interrogation shack with the HUMINT team right now.

Kiley sighs and shakes her head.

KILEY
I think I know what's going on. This happened to me before.

ZANE
What did?

KILEY
Someone comes in claiming to be someone else, usually a relative, trying to make some cash.

Kiley sighs.

KILEY
Thank you for your time, sergeant.

Zane nods and Kiley walks away. Sergeant Major grins at Zane.

SERGEANT MAJOR
That went well.

ZANE
I really don't appreciate having a female trying to tell me how to do my job.

SERGEANT MAJOR
She was just doing her job. Besides, I think you won. She seemed pretty defeated.

ZANE
Yeah, I don't believe in using kid gloves for female soldiers.

SERGEANT MAJOR
You know, I always wished that I had gone for the smart ones when I was young, instead of just chasing anything in a skirt.

ZANE
Where did that come from?

SERGEANT MAJOR
I'm just saying.

ZANE
Uh huh. I bet you were a hard one to keep up with during your skirt-chasing days.

                    SERGEANT MAJOR
          From what I've heard, you probably would've been a worthy
          competitor.

                    ZANE
          Sergeant Major, those days are long gone for me.

                    SERGEANT MAJOR
          Thinking about settling down now?

                    ZANE
          No. I'm thinking about becoming a grouchy hermit.

                    SERGEANT MAJOR
          Becoming one? That's what you need to grow out of.

EXT. OUTDOOR WEIGHT ROOM—NIGHT

Kiley is on the bench press and Zane is using the seated row machine. Zane watches Kiley struggling under the weight that she is benching. Sergeant Major does dips in the background, watching both.

                    (MORE)

CHILDREN'S FICTION WINNERS

1 Peggy Tromblay
Dousman WI
2 Kimberley Foster
Vancouver BC Canada
3 Donna Louise Watkinson
Kitchener ON Canada
4 James P. Day
Yuba City CA
5 Judy Hopkins
Coronado CA
6 Heidi Derks-Rehmann
Spruce MI
7 David A. Norris
Scappoose OR
8 Laura Resau
Fort Collins CO
9 Aaron Reynolds
Fox River Grove IL
10 Muriel Harris Weinstein
Great Neck NY
11 Karen Addison Picciani
New York NY
12 Rebecca O. Hayes
Scottsdale AZ
13 Sherry North
Sunrise FL
14 Linda Marie
Clearwater MN
15 Carol N. Flaherty
Wrentham MA
16 Laurie Calkhoven
New York NY
17 Andrew Beahrs
Berkeley CA
18 Mark Loth
Pataskala OH
19 Mary McCarthy-Tapp
Thorton CO
20 Margaret Skipworth
Hull United Kingdom
21 Anne Allison
Bloomfield Hills MI
22 Marnie Brooks
Cary NC
23 Robert J. Miller
San Jose CA
24 Michele Peterson
Fresno CA
25 Mary E. Durham
Austin TX
26 Lucy Crisetig
Mississauga ON Canada
27 Jan Sherbin
Cincinnati OH
28 John Nicholson
Oak Park IL
29 T.S. Bjornstad
Clawson MI
30 Ellen L. Ramsey
Downingtown PA
31 Wendy Hogarth
Bala ON Canada
32 Stephanie Milbourn
San Angelo TX
33 Louis M. DiGiuseppe
Syracuse NY
34 Jan Carrington
Abilene TX

35 Fox Carlton Hughes
Dayton NV
36 Lana Bee
Phoenix AZ
37 Lin Johns
Calgary AB Canada
38 Jessie Churchill
East Providence RI
39 Roxyanne Young
San Diego CA
40 Dana Konop
Canton GA
41 Tricia Orr
Warner NH
42 Laurie A. Jacobs
Swampscott MA
43 Jennifer B. Jones
Homer NY
44 Annie-Laurie Lang
Fredericksburg TX
45 Jacqueline Guest
Bragg Creek AB Canada
46 Christine Richmond
Port Coquitlam BC Canada
47 Karen Beaumont
San Martin CA
48 Donna Gephart
Jupiter FL
49 Isabelle Southcott
Powell River BC Canada
50 B.J. Appelgren
Charles Town WV
51 Wendy Greenley
Blue Bell PA
52 Leanne Currie-McGhee
Norfolk VA
53 Karen Schulz
Stillwater MN
54 Pat Shagoury
Dover NH
55 Robert J. Miller
San Jose CA
56 Eve Begley Kiehm
Fox Island WA
57 Donna Surgenor Reames
Charleston SC
58 Josephine Nobisso
Quogue NY
59 Karen Gideon
Truckee CA
60 Teresa Novacek
Eagan MN
61 Katrina Papanastassiou
Stow MA
62 Lois Avrick
Delray Beach FL
63 Maribel Martinez Font
North Miami Beach FL
64 Richelle Putnam
Meridian MS
65 Cathleen Burnham
Pittsford NY
66 Christine E. Shumway
Higden AR
67 Judy E. Bryan
Madison WI
68 Carole Connor Bargelt
Clemson SC

69 Martha R. Fehl
Brookville IN
70 Cyndi Struven
Goleta CA
71 Elizabeth Cooper
Danville CA
72 Fran Cannon Slayton
Charlottesville VA
73 Sandra A. Heffington
Avondale AZ
74 Nicole Vincenti
Brick NJ
75 Syrl Ann Kazlo
Fort Ann NY
76 B.L. Valentine
Waynesboro VA
77 Robin Alberg
Seattle WA
78 Chrissy K. McVay
Little Switzerland NC
79 Laurie Heimbigner
Pullman WA
80 Loretta Kellogg Adrienne Canull
Pleasant Valley NY
81 Pamela Greer
Seatac WA
82 Sandy Baldwin
Kelowna BC Canada
83 Tami Casias
Sonoma CA
84 Geraldine Ann Marshall
Paducah KY
85 Jean Reagan
Salt Lake City UT
86 Patricia Moore
Midlothian IL
87 Andrea J. Robinson
Queens NY
88 Adele Portnoy
Boynton Beach FL
89 Cheryl Horn
Halfmoon Bay BC Canada
90 Lorianne E. Wright-Gumm
Glendale AZ
91 Laura G. Black
Hoover AL
92 Holly Niner
Fort Wayne IN
93 Jody S. Thomas
Arvada CO
94 Barnel Bragg
Anacortes WA
95 Heather Hall
Coquitlam BC Canada
96 Amy Leask
Cambridge ON Canada
97 Debra Henry
Ceduna SA Australia
98 Judith Gussmann
Berkeley CA
99 Gayle Lockwood
Salem OR
100 Lindsay Eland
Breckenridge CO

FEATURE ARTICLE WINNERS

1 Linda Bren
  Rockville MD
2 Barbara Anton
  Sarasota FL
3 Jennifer Lacy
  Minneola FL
4 Christy Heitger-Casbon
  Noblesville IN
5 Laura Kinsel
  Mountain View CA
6 John Moir
  Santa Cruz CA
7 Robert Kirchgassner
  Cincinnati OH
8 Amy Puccinelli
  Danville CA
9 Barbara Anton
  Sarasota FL
10 Louis J. Giamelle
  Dededo Guam
11 Wilma M. Wagner
  Sacramento CA
12 Robert B. Robeson
  Lincoln NE
13 Gayla Dease
  Orange Park FL
14 Jennifer Lacy
  Minneola FL
15 Judi Brown
  Rising Sun MD
16 Evan E. Filby
  Idaho Falls ID
17 Janet Park
  Seattle WA
18 Gayla Dease
  Orange Park FL
19 Gayla Dease
  Orange Park FL
20 Kimberly Rau
  Olympia WA
21 Connie Young
  Westminster CO
22 Michael White
  Plainsboro NJ
23 Jennifer Lacy
  Minneola FL
24 Linda Hagen Miller
  Spokane WA
25 Thomas Frey
  Wayne MI
26 Anthony Head
  Los Angeles CA
27 Sherrie Dulworth
  Mount Kisco NY
28 Elizabeth Walker
  Germantown TN
29 Burton Milward, Jr.
  Fairfield IA
30 Kimberley C. Kalicky
  Portland ME
31 Linda Fisher
  Sedalia MO
32 Christy Heitger-Casbon
  Noblesville IN
33 Krysten Weller
  Grand Blanc MI
34 Julia Browne
  Kitchener ON Canada

35 Susan Hamilton
  Spokane WA
36 Susan Hamilton
  Spokane WA
37 Jayne Freeman
  Gladstone OR
38 John Gorman
  Miami FL
39 Corrie Lynne Player
  Cedar City UT
40 Gail Robertson
  Richmond VA
41 Lisa McCubbin
  Naperville IL
42 Amy Wideman
  Chicago IL
43 Richard A. Kuffel
  Plymouth MN
44 Juliett K. Yoon
  Salinas CA
45 Kimberly Kennedy
  Covington KY
46 Jayne Freeman
  Gladstone OR
47 Butch Holcombe
  Acworth GA
48 Ted J. Conigliaro
  Naples FL
49 Gail Martin
  Charlotte NC
50 James R. Sajo
  APO AE Italy
51 Tandy Ringoringo
  Houston TX
52 Kay Rios
  Fort Collins CO
53 Andrea M. Chenoweth
  Pascagoula MS
54 Richard Thayer
  Thomasville NC
55 Jean Reidy
  Littleton CO
56 Linda E. Allen
  Stillwater OK
57 Francine Latil
  Arlington MA
58 Sandra McLeod Humphrey
  Annandale MN
59 Melissa Kent Parnell
  Branson MO
60 Stephanie Wells
  Toronto ON Canada
61 Peggy L. Ellis
  Black Mountain NC
62 Sherrie Dulworth
  Mount Kisco NY
63 James L. Embrey
  Rineyville KY
64 Charles Culbertson
  Staunton VA
65 Margaret Jones
  Providenciales AB Turks and Caicos Islands
66 Karen A. Fiordaliso
  Blackwood NJ
67 Dale Leatherman
  Slatyfork WV
68 Judy Penz Sheluk
  Landing ON Canada

69 Timothy Glass
  Albuquerque NM
70 Angie Still
  Denham Springs LA
71 Suzanna Quintana
  Sheridan WY
72 Mariana Williams
  Sunset Beach CA
73 Lizabeth Peak
  Springfield MO
74 Laura Wasson Warfel
  Thompsonville IL
75 Corrie Lynne Player
  Cedar City UT
76 Barbara Elizabeth Rehder
  Wellington New Zealand
77 Linda Fisher
  Sedalia MO
78 Susan Fishman
  Atlanta GA
79 Ana Maria Nezol
  Salem OR
80 Mary Kion
  Kennewick WA
81 Cissy Moody
  Cloverdale AL
82 Robert L. Shoop
  Colorado Springs CO
83 Terry K. League
  Oxford MS
84 Karen T. Pemberton
  Dayton OH
85 Stephanie Starr
  Irvine CA
86 Lisa Snider
  Ojai CA
87 Kathleen Vestal Logan
  Gulf Breeze FL
88 Christine Genovese
  La Haye-Pesnel France
89 Barbara Sharik
  Jones LA
90 Kristy Dark
  Ojai CA
91 Riley St. James
  San Clemente CA
92 Joanne Bamberger
  Bethesda MD
93 Joanne Bamberger
  Bethesda MD
94 Jenifer Lacey
  Minneola FL
95 Camille Singleton
  Wabash IN
96 Robert L. Shoop
  Colorado Springs CO
97 Sharon Edmonds
  Tucson AZ
98 Martha R. Fehl
  Brookville IN
99 Christy Potter
  Union NJ
100 Riley N. Kelly
  Excel AL

77

GENRE SHORT STORY WINNERS

1 Margaret E. Anderson
 Houston TX
2 Christina Hamlett
 Pasadena CA
3 Don George
 Aiken SC
4 John M. Prophet
 Harwich MA
5 Laura Preble
 La Mesa CA
6 Bonnie D. Taylor
 Gig Harbor WA
7 Mary Etta Bersig
 Indianapolis IN
8 Kathleen M. Curry
 Blue Mountain Lake NY
9 Theresa Wood
 Heisson WA
10 Patricia Edmisten
 Fresno CA
11 Charles Meierdiercks
 Corvallis OR
12 Alesia Kunz
 Berkley CA
13 Donald Helin
 Newport PA
14 M.P. Barker
 East Longmeadow MA
15 James Steed
 Little Rock AR
16 Thea Ramsay
 Paia HI
17 Wayne Borden
 Whitinsville MA
18 M. Marko, SFO
 Chicago IL
19 Robert Mayer
 Santa Fe NM
20 Deborah Nold
 Yuba City CA
21 Shirlee Matheson
 Calgary AL Canada
22 Mike Coleman
 Atlanta GA
23 Veronica Dale
 Mount Clemens MI
24 Tima Smith
 Pomfret Center CT
25 Marilyn H. Collins
 Rogers AR
26 Keith Lawrence
 Spring TX
27 Coleen Steele
 Bowmanville ON Canada
28 Susanne Schubarsky
 Villach Austria
29 Corey J. Robins
 Van Nuys CA
30 Morton M. Rumberg
 Rancho Cordova CA
31 Lorraine Buck
 Charlottetown PE Canada
32 Susan Bennett Lobo
 Thompsons Station TN
33 David E. Hughes
 Louisville CO
34 Jim Fant
 Dallas TX

35 Jan Kniesly
 Overland Park KS
36 Melanie Marks
 Eliot ME
37 Henry E. Hack
 Miller Place NY
38 Nancy Swanner
 Athens AL
39 Bryan Gilmer
 Durham NC
40 Marla Todd
 Orangevale CA
41 Don Abbott
 Hudson MA
42 Jamie Hamilton
 Allentown PA
43 John E. Lewis
 Orem UT
44 Kristy Dark
 Ojai CA
45 Vonda Garett
 Troy AL
46 Kristin Mascio
 Redondo Beach CA
47 John P. Kinghorn
 Essex Junction VT
48 Bruce Robinson
 Junction City KS
49 Mary Mahan
 Tucson AZ
50 Geraldine Bass
 Olathe KS
51 Mignonne D. Davis
 Lexington MA
52 Brett Yamada
 Englewood CO
53 Nicholas DeRosa
 Coram NY
54 Lisa Cobb Sabatini
 Exeter PA
55 Milovan Katanic
 Hermitage PA
56 Steve Donoho
 Chantilly VA
57 Sean Guiggey
 Lewiston ME
58 Bruce Krause
 Seattle WA
59 Carol Robinson
 New York NY
60 Darla Dee Burris
 Alliance OH
61 Scott Andrews
 Florence AZ
62 C.L. Frost
 Bantam CT
63 Chick Lang
 Laurel MS
64 Jim Norton
 New Berlin WI
65 Sunny Frazier
 Lemoore CA
66 David Surrett
 Columbia SC
67 Bruce Graham
 Winter Park FL
68 Ann Chandler
 New Westminster BC Canada

69 Mary Caraker
 San Francisco CA
70 Julia Nichols
 Chillicothe OH
71 Jeremy Morphis
 Bryant AR
72 Tom Lavagnino
 Los Angeles CA
73 Adriana Civita
 Delray Beach FL
74 John Lewis
 Bloomfield MO
75 Valerie Wheat
 Loxahatchee FL
76 Michelle Hoffman
 Fountain Hills AZ
77 David Wainland
 Boca Raton FL
78 Susan Endow
 Carpinteria CA
79 Francis Fiskey, Jr.
 Carol City FL
80 Ted K. Ernst
 Stevensville MT
81 Don George
 Aiken SC
82 Doug Grubich
 Ordway CO
83 Joshua Lynch
 Slidell LA
84 Natalie Wilder
 Delaware OH
85 Pete Frohn
 Columbus GA
86 Miriam Goodspeed
 Palm Harbor FL
87 Gil Howard
 East Concord NY
88 Sharon Skinner
 Indianapolis IN
89 Leslee C. Breene
 Denver CO
90 Maria Riley
 Lake Mary FL
91 Paul A. Barra
 Reidville SC
92 Michael S. Strickland
 Ashville AL
93 Jean Cozby
 Redmond WA
94 Linda Bilodeau
 Bonita Springs FL
95 C.L. Frost
 Bantam CT
96 Ronald M. Penczak
 Salem NH
97 Sheila Boldon
 Cody WY
98 Eugene Orlando
 Seffner FL
99 J.L. Wong
 Bakersfield CA
100 William J. Cowley
 East Hampton NY

INSPIRATIONAL WRITING WINNERS

1 Mal King
Santa Paula CA
2 Maria-Elena Castegna
Jamaica NY
3 Lisa Audette
Castleton VT
4 Tom Bentley
Watsonville CA
5 Amy Hagberg
Buffalo MN
6 Annette Langer
Pleasanton CA
7 Amy Shane
Bakersfield CA
8 Judith J. Coyle
Blue Island IL
9 Evelyn Echols
Chicago IL
10 Donna Surgenor Reames
Charleston SC
11 Annette Langer
Pleasanton CA
12 James L. Embrey
Rineyville KY
13 Duane A. Gallop
New York NY
14 Linda Steele
Midlothian TX
15 Carol Heilman
Hendersonville NC
16 David E. Coulter
Mabelvale AR
17 Teri Blair
Minneapolis MN
18 Concetta Ciccozzi Doucette
South Windsor CT
19 Danny David Davison
Toledo OH
20 Duane A. Gallop
New York, NY
21 C. Bruce Moore
Geneseo IL
22 Rev. Denise Glavan
Littleton CO
23 Maeann Jasa
Wahoo NE
24 Scott Eldredge
Troy MI
25 John Williams
Tucson AZ
26 Tamalyn Kralman
Bellingham WA
27 Scott Bork/Rhonda Duncan
Greenville SC
28 J. Graham Ducker
Oshawa ON Canada
29 Lana Danielle Jacobson
Johannesburg South Africa
30 Sue Boltz
Cuyahoga Falls OH
31 Julie Pruitt
Saint Louis MO
32 Thomas J. Bundy, Sr.
Rogersville TN
33 Barbara N. Varma
Santa Ana CA
34 Adam Benezra
Danvers MA

35 Beatrice Fishback
APO AE United Kingdom
36 Frances Allen White
New Orleans LA
37 Adriana DiNardo
Brooklyn NY
38 Laura F. Tutt
Wasilla AK
39 Rebecca Van Ness
Corona CA
40 Andrea Theisen
Uvalde TX
41 Katherine Bynum
Suceava Romania
42 Walter Ansel Strong, III
Dundee IL
43 Laurel Karry
Carlisle ON Canada
44 Shirley Radin
West Bloomfield MI
45 Sherman Richard Shook
Slater IA
46 Bessie Michael
La Jose PA
47 Ellen Notbohm
Portland OR
48 Leon Mentzer
Decatur IL
49 Veronica Pinckard
Valencia CA
50 Jo Ann S. Barefoot
Westerville OH
51 Dorothy S. Jones
Ashland KY
52 Diane Hobaugh
Santa Rosa CA
53 Dori A. Klass
Carlsbad CA
54 Barbara Fox
Acworth, GA
55 Scott Morales
Fort Wayne IN
56 Chuck Bennett
Los Fresnos TX
57 Fran Bauman
Saginaw MI
58 Mary E. Vela
San Antonio TX
59 Deborah Solomon
Rochester NY
60 Art Lester
Torremolinos Spain
61 Jane F. White
Houston TX
62 James Crosby
Lumberport WV
63 Holmes Brannon
Woodland Park CO
64 L. Ann Eynon
Villanova PA
65 Dawn Kirk
Nashville TN
66 Daniel Leonard
Oak Ridge TN
67 Susan J. Haas
Mill Hall PA
68 Richard Thayer
Thomasville NC

69 Lucille Maurice Maistros
Havre De Grace MD
70 Charles Bennett
Los Fresnos TX
71 Robbie Jeanne Bayler
Orlando FL
72 Janet Eckles
Orlando FL
73 Loren A. Clough
Oxnard CA
74 Irene Leland
Saint Louis MO
75 Nanette Clark
Edwardsville IL
76 Anna Green Hickman
Killen AL
77 Terri Tiffany
Clermont FL
78 James F. O'Callaghan
Maple Valley WA
79 Heather Fuller
Westminster CA
80 Lois Jean Lee
Kenmore, NY
81 Angela Cannon-Crothers
Prattsburg NY
82 Connie F. Miller
Kihei HI
83 Reneé Cassidy
Simpsonville SC
84 Ellen E. Gee
Saint Cloud FL
85 Dave Wiley
Chesterland OH
86 Debbie Michael
Mount Airy MD
87 Margaret Terry
Burlington ON Canada
88 Samantha Duclouw Waltz
Lake Oswego OR
89 Rev. Lyn G. Brakeman
Gloucester MA
90 Joseph White
Los Angeles CA
91 Edie Hudson
Greenfield IN
92 Winifred S. Erickson
Scottsdale AZ
93 Brad Paulson
Spokane WA
94 Carol Heilman
Hendersonville NC
95 Mary Andonian
Tualatin OR
96 Marlene Salcher
San Antonio TX
97 Dorothy Giman-Small
Pontiac MI
98 Fiona Cole
Altadena CA
99 Al S. Morrison
Sulphur Springs TX
100 Annette S. Bogard
Derby KS

MAINSTREAM/LITERARY SHORT STORY WINNERS

1 Teresa Little
Jacksonville FL
2 Cassandra Key
Christoval TX
3 Richelle Putnam
Meridian MS
4 Susan Paturzo
Ranchos De Taos NM
5 Brenda A. Morris
Palmyra VA
6 Barbara L. Porter
Anchorage AK
7 Michael Clements
Texas City TX
8 N.M. Patino
Green Valley AZ
9 William S. Frankl
Wynnewood PA
10 Aideen Bugler
Belmar NJ
11 Dorothy C. Snyder
Jefferson City TN
12 Marcia Sandground
Osprey FL
13 Kathryn Mattingly
Elk Grove CA
14 Neroli Cochrane
Shepparton Victoria Australia
15 Cathy Howard
Grand Island NE
16 Heather Gansel
New Canaan CT
17 Ruth P. Watson
Atlanta GA
18 John Fite Rebrovick
Nashville TN
19 Loretta Kellogg
Pleasant Valley NY
20 Steven Hagy
Clovis CA
21 Amy Lucas
Beverly Hills CA
22 Barbara Bitela
Antelope CA
23 Bernice Warner
San Marcos CA
24 Suzanne Schryver
Merrimack NH
25 Charles V. Brown
Millersville MD
26 Riley N. Kelly
Excel AL
27 Debra F. Nickell
Lexington KY
28 Jean Jenkins
San Diego CA
29 Danielle Thorne
Bartlett TN
30 Hanako Brown
Houston TX
31 Pamela Edwards
New York NY
32 Patricia A. Bennett
Hagatna Guam
33 Stephanie Conn
Long Beach CA
34 O.J. Bryson
Hixson TN

35 Laurie B. Moore
Chester NH
36 Maureen Hourihan
Brewster MA
37 Johanna Bilbo Staton
Collingswood NJ
38 Elaine Carr Spain
Montgomery AL
39 Carrie R. Donovan
Baltimore MD
40 Julie Kalbfleisch
Waterloo ON Canada
41 Barbara Anton
Sarasota FL
42 Debra H. Snider
Henderson NV
43 Neil Naft
Toronto ON Canada
44 Lana Kyle
Sevierville TN
45 Nancy J. Kauffman
Fleetwood PA
46 Kimberly Lengyel
San Diego CA
47 Dr. Derrick C. R. Hurlin
Pretoria South Africa
48 Nancy Chloe Lewis
Cumming GA
49 Linda K. Rettstatt
Southaven MS
50 Christina Strick
Keswick VA
51 Kirsten Mickelwait Bickford
Rutherford CA
52 Kirsten Mickelwait Bickford
Rutherford CA
53 Barbara Villemez
Las Cruces NM
54 William T. Milburn
Winter Haven FL
55 Deborah Poore
Scarborough ME
56 Yvonne M. Anderson
New Philadelphia OH
57 Lisa Allard
Collinsville CT
58 Kate Dore
San Luis Obispo CA
59 Ann Wuthrich
Sandy UT
60 Ann Brittain
Mount Vernon WA
61 Kiera Stewart
Annandale VA
62 Linda Lucretia Shuler
San Antonio TX
63 Gabriela Blandy
Salisbury United Kingdom
64 Willa Schmidt
Madison WI
65 Susan Ryan
Louisville KY
66 Nancy Rustici
Pawcatuck CT
67 Annie Slessman
Edwardsburg MI
68 Joyce Simmons
Richland MS

69 Danae Lealie
Canal Fulton OH
70 Christine Mattice
Hartville OH
71 Dan Olsen
Chandler AZ
72 Jack O'Connor
Chimacum WA
73 Ruth Laczavics
Willcox AZ
74 David Gaughan
Auckland New Zealand
75 Faye E. Arcand
Okanagan Falls BC Canada
76 Eugene Orlando
Seffner FL
77 Meika McClurg
Toronto ON Canada
78 Michael Stockman
Boston MA
79 Jennifer Anderson
Waite Park MN
80 Daniel K. Egan
Mount Laurel NJ
81 Michael W. Drwiega
Wilmette IL
82 Lee Wheeler
Newhall CA
83 Maureen R. Neely
Scottsdale AZ
84 Melissa Jackson Brister
Panama City Beach FL
85 K.J.W. Wilyums
Hempstead NY
86 Deborah Mantella
Alpharetta GA
87 J.G. Walker
Chickasaw AL
88 Maureen W. Bellis
Saint Paul MN
89 Lana Kyle
Sevierville TN
90 Cynthia L. Orlowski
West Chester OH
91 Linda Rossi
Andover MA
92 Melody Graves
Mansfield TX
93 Michael Marsh
Liverpool NY
94 Joe Reyes
Long Island City NY
95 Christopher Elliott
Etta MS
96 Marianne Lonsdale
Oakland CA
97 Rachel Goldman
Dresden ME
98 D.J. Van Kirk
Dearborn MI
99 Patricia Bailey
Klamath Falls OR
100 Austin Alexis
New York NY

MEMOIR/PERSONAL ESSAY WINNERS

1 Lori Loson
Littleton CO
2 Jill V. Svoboda
Nobleton FL
3 Barbara B. Amberger Scott
Dobson NC
4 Tracy Gary
New York NY
5 Sarah A. Ongiri
Bethlehem PA
6 Thomas M. Driscoll
Avon OH
7 Randall H. Nunn
Sherman TX
8 Cullen Dorn
Melbourne FL
9 Patrick Palmer
San Diego CA
10 Morton M. Rumberg
Rancho Cordova CA
11 Courtney Lichterman
Los Angeles CA
12 Seetha Narayan
Fort Collins CO
13 Anita
London United Kingdom
14 James Patterson
Washington D.C.
15 Joan Grindley
Fort Myers FL
16 Xujun Eberlein
Wayland MA
17 Natasha Leigh Yates
Red Wing MN
18 Bruce Graham
Winter Park FL
19 Paula Younger
New York NY
20 Karen Albright Lin
Longmont CO
21 Lutz Braum
San Francisco CA
22 Nancy Tupper Ling
Walpole MA
23 Cecilie Scott
Duvall WA
24 H.G. Don Mercer
Virginia Beach VA
25 Becky Browder
Jacksonville AL
26 Hugo W. Matson
Gansevoort NY
27 Cindy O'Brien
Vashon WA
28 Kyle Minor
Columbus OH
29 Kirk Blackard
Houston TX
30 Benjamin Carp
Marco Island FL
31 Da Chen
Highland NY
32 Robin Schoenthaler
Arlington MA
33 Janet Feldman
Las Vegas NV
34 Anne-Marie Gallagher
Chicago IL

35 Catherine Bergart
Morristown NJ
36 Janet Koppers Wichmann
Orland Park IL
37 Rebecca Boissonneault
Alvin TX
38 Lesley Pallathumadom
Union City NJ
39 Sarah Green
San Jose CA
40 Daniela Gibson
San Francisco CA
41 Kathryn Presley
Bryan TX
42 Lynn Wallen
Windsor WI
43 Judith J. Coyle
Blue Island IL
44 Josephine D. Jasmund
Wells MI
45 Joseph Curreri
Philadelphia PA
46 Jay Sanger
Hereford AZ
47 Shannon McFarlin
Paris TN
48 Charles Culbertson
Staunton VA
49 Alda Sigmundsdottir
Reykjavik Iceland
50 Zibby Schwarzman
New York NY
51 Darrell P. Thorpe
Pinetop AZ
52 Olga Gladky Verro
High Point NC
53 Jack Fles
South Salem NY
54 Alyson Mead
Los Angeles CA
55 Jean H. Mohr
Santa Clara CA
56 Lawrence Carrino
Pembroke Pines FL
57 Felicia Graber
Saint Louis MO
58 Rebecca Van Ness
Corona CA
59 Kathy J. McCarthy
Bicknell UT
60 Kirk Blackard
Houston TX
61 Paul Woodward
Katy TX
62 Arlene Uslander
Glenview IL
63 Peggy Jeager
Keene NH
64 Jacqueline Dooley
Eddyville NY
65 Sandy Wiles
Palatine IL
66 Ken Fouts
Batavia OH
67 Mary Helen Straker
Bonita Springs FL
68 Helene Barnes
Palo Alto CA

69 Sandra A. Heffinton
Avondale-Goodyear AZ
70 Nees Firebaugh
Escondido CA
71 Sandra A. Heffington
Avondale-Goodyear AZ
72 Jan Sherbin
Cincinnati OH
73 Sara McNulty
Staten Island NY
74 Tom Piantanida
Redwood City CA
75 Jan Sherbin
Cincinnati OH
76 Mary McEwan
Hoquiam WA
77 Ros McIntosh
Alameda CA
78 Allan C. Stover
Ellicott City MD
79 George Jones
Leeds AL
80 Robin Schoenthaler
Arlington MA
81 Patricia A. Tyler
Cotati CA
82 Erec Toso
Tucson AZ
83 Camille Cuaumano
San Francisco CA
84 Ruth McCallum
New Orleans LA
85 Claire Yezbak Fadden
Chula Vista CA
86 Patti Charron
Louisville KY
87 Joyce Seymore Smith
Marion AR
88 Oliver French
Brooktondale NY
89 Crystal Stango
Lakewood NJ
90 Jean Spencer
Green Valley AZ
91 David Horne
APO AE United States of America
92 Edith Jacobs
Sarasota FL
93 Julenne Deitrick Barshop
Schertz TX
94 Sumita Rachapudi
Cary NC
95 Andrew H. Johnson
Aurora CO
96 Amy Wink Krebs
Albany NY
97 Sally Angelino
Sandy OR
98 Alexander Efimento
Bernex Switzerland
99 Frank Thornburgh
Walnut Creek CA
100 Deborah G. Kearns
Mechanicsburg PA

NON-RHYMING POETRY WINNERS

1 Christo Pretorius
Pretoria South Africa
2 Lori Romero
Santa Fe NM
3 Chandi J. Wyant
Louisville CO
4 Maria Ercilla
Los Angeles CA
5 Ronald Wertheim
Fort Lauderdale FL
6 Maria Ercilla
Los Angeles CA
7 Doug Thiele
Norfolk VA
8 Lynn Wallen
Windsor WI
9 Crystalee Calderwood
Altoona PA
10 Bruce W. Niedt
Cherry Hill NJ
11 Patricia Dreyfus
Corona Del Mar CA
12 Maria Ercilla
Los Angeles CA
13 Chandi J. Wyant
Louisville CO
14 Sheila Murphy
Portland CT
15 Cristine A. Gruber
Riverside CA
16 Danielle Thierry
Riverton NJ
17 Jean Coulombre
Medfield MA
18 Maria Ercilla
Los Angeles CA
19 Bruce Rolf
Livingston TX
20 Joan Higuchi
West Islip NY
21 Christo Pretorius
Pretoria South Africa
22 Patti J. Kurtz
Sawyer ND
23 Arturo Cantu Hernandez
San Antonio TX
24 Bill Hinthorn
Palm Springs CA
25 N. Colwell Snell
Salt Lake City UT
26 Doug Thiele
Norfolk VA
27 N. Colwell Snell
Salt Lake City UT
28 Joan Higuchi
West Islip NY
29 Elaine Romp
Excelsior Springs MO
30 Maria Ercilla
Los Angeles CA
31 Martha Modena Vertreace-Doody
Chicago IL
32 Senecia Wilson
Fresno CA
33 Deborah Naybor
Alden NY
34 Tom K. Wagner
Phoenix AZ

35 Deborah DeNicola
Boston MA
36 Darlene Estlow
Heisson WA
37 Doug Thiele
Norfolk VA
38 Robert Daseler
Davis CA
39 Bonnie Wilks
Arlington TX
40 Bonnie Wilks
Arlington TX
41 Martha Modena Vertreace-Doody
Chicago IL
42 Melinda DePorte
Cambridge MA
43 Norma Lipp
Kalispell MT
44 Patti Kurtz
Sawyer ND
45 Mariah Huehner
Hastings on Hudson NY
46 Mary Smith Pritchard
Midlothian TX
47 Gloria Masterson-Richardson
Rockport MA
48 Bonnie Wilks
Arlington TX
49 Jake Langthorn
Arcadia OK
50 Max Redfire
East Falmouth MA
51 Maria Ercilla
Los Angeles CA
52 Shirley Smith Wilbert
Columbia MO
53 Sheri DiPrince
Pueblo CO
54 Sheri Furgason
Mount Vernon MO
55 Martha Modena Vertreace-Doody
Chicago IL
56 Carol Roth
Wenonah NJ
57 Wendi L. Sims
Chicago IL
58 J.R. Turek
East Meadow NY
59 Wendi L. Sims
Chicago IL
60 Elizabeth Lowe
Martinsburg WV
61 Nancy A. Patterson
Chatham MA
62 John J. Candelaria
Corrales NM
63 Anne-Marie Legan
Herrin IL
64 Cristina Ferrari-Logan
Lafayette CA
65 Andrea Meyer
Fort Drum NY
66 Andrea Meyer
Fort Drum NY
67 Andrea Meyer
Fort Drum NY
68 Pamela Phillips
Olympia WA

69 Martha Moffett
Lake Worth FL
70 Amy Wink Krebs
Albany NY
71 Nancy Tupper Ling
Walpole MA
72 Marissa Bell
Danville CA
73 Andrea Meyer
Fort Drum NY
74 Andrea Theisen
Uvalde TX
75 Debbie L. Davis
Kingsport TN
76 Laura Hluska
Munster IN
77 Laura Hluska
Munster IN
78 Kristin Gosline
Tampa FL
79 Joan Peck Arnold
Gloucester MA
80 Sneha Madhavan-Reese
Ypsilanti MI
81 Sarah French
Colorado Springs CO
82 Elizabeth Lowe
Martinsburg WV
83 Gloria D. Conly
Winchester KY
84 Sheri Furgason
Mount Vernon MO
85 Neil Nason
Temple Terrace FL
86 Dawn DiPrince
Pueblo CO
87 Shirley Smith Wilbert
Columbia MO
88 Mary Smith Pritchard
Midlothian TX
89 Laura Purdie Salas
Maple Grove MN
90 Joy Turner-Price
Greenville OH
91 Maja Zmyslowski Frank
Salinas CA
92 Lucy Ireland Smiley
Birmingham AL
93 Darlene Estlow
Heisson WA
94 Ronda Lawson
Castro Valley CA
95 Roy Reichle
Bellevue NE
96 Beth C. Ford
Portland OR
97 Lori Romero
Santa Fe NM
98 J.R. Turek
East Meadow NY
99 LaSharndra Clark
Chicago IL
100 Nancy A. Patterson
Chatham MA

RHYMING POETRY WINNERS

1 Anna Evans
Hainesport NJ
2 Will Clemens
Cincinnati OH
3 Tryna Zeedyk
Aurora IL
4 Ellen Elizabeth
Bremerton WA
5 Douglas W. Clark
Albuquerque NM
6 Douglas W. Clark
Albuquerque NM
7 Fred Barrett
Portland OR
8 Douglas W. Clark
Albuquerque NM
9 Will Clemens
Cincinnati OH
10 Verna Lee Hinegardner
Hot Springs National Park AR
11 Walter A. Kuciej
Seattle WA
12 Sarah Singer
Seattle WA
13 N. Colwell Snell
Salt Lake City UT
14 Sarah Singer
Seattle WA
15 J.M. Ferguson, Jr.
Tigard OR
16 Sarah Singer
Seattle WA
17 Robert Daseler
Davis CA
18 Jendi Reiter
Northampton MA
19 Sarah Singer
Seattle WA
20 Melissa Cannon
Nashville TN
21 Sheila A. Murphy
Portland CT
22 Robert Daseler
Davis CA
23 Ms. Troy Parker Farr
San Luis Obispo CA
24 Melissa Cannon
Nashville TN
25 Sarah Singer
Seattle WA
26 Melissa Balmain
Blacksburg VA
27 Andrew B. Pierce
Miami FL
28 Sarah Singer
Seattle WA
29 N. Colwell Snell
Salt Lake City UT
30 Amy Jordan
Los Angeles CA
31 Marian Wilson
Tucson AZ
32 David Swanson
Lincoln CA
33 B. Hulick
North Truro MA
34 Roy Reichle
Bellevue NE

35 Carla Conley
Newmarket NH
36 Maureen Cannon
Ridgewood NJ
37 Sheila A. Murphy
Portland CT
38 Michelle Pell
Fort Stewart GA
39 Sheila A. Murphy
Portland CT
40 Alli Hammond
Cincinnati OH
41 Robert Daseler
Davis CA
42 Richard Coan
Tucson AZ
43 Melissa Cannon
Nashville TN
44 Cameron Mount
Cambridge MA
45 Robert Daseler
Davis CA
46 C.L. Frost
Bantam CT
47 Gordon Plank
Edgartown MA
48 David Swanson
Lincoln CA
49 Robert Daseler
Davis CA
50 Suellen Wedmore
Rockport MA
51 Roy Robbins
Cartersville VA
52 Robert Daseler
Davis CA
53 Rohana McCormack
Indianapolis IN
54 Melissa Cannon
Nashville TN
55 Darlene Dauphin
Missouri City TX
56 Robert Daseler
Davis CA
57 Von S. Bourland
Happy TX
58 Anna Amatuzio
New York NY
59 Robert Daseler
Davis CA
60 Elaine Ambrose Romano
McCall ID
61 Helen L. Gillies
New York NY
62 Roy Reichle
Bellevue NE
63 Jendi Reiter
Northampton MA
64 C.L. Frost
Bantam CT
65 William A. Holt
Fort Worth TX
66 C.L. Frost
Bantam CT
67 Melissa Cannon
Nashville TN
68 Nancy Jean Carrigan
Warrenville IL

69 Michael Miller
Seattle WA
70 Rohana McCormack
Indianapolis IN
71 Yun Di Yi
Brooklyn NY
72 Rochelle Brener
Sedona AZ
73 Andrew B. Pierce
Miami FL
74 J.M. Ferguson
Tigard OR
75 Ronda Lawson
Castro Valley CA
76 Bryan Gilmer
Durham NC
77 Sandy Fink
Dowling Park FL
78 Sydnea Miles
Hinesville GA
79 Sydnea Miles
Hinesville GA
80 Marian Wilson
Tucson AZ
81 Michael R. Burch
Nashville TN
82 R.H. Peat
Auburn CA
83 Fred J. Miller
Topeka KS
84 Lynn Veach Sadler
Sanford NC
85 William A. Holt
Fort Worth TX
86 William Batcher
Calverton NY
87 N. Colwell Snell
Salt Lake City UT
88 Sabrina Kahren
Carpentersville IL
89 Yvonne Nunn
Hermleigh TX
90 Mildred M. Marshall
Vienna WV
91 Pamala S. Loy
Los Angeles CA
92 Barbara Cline
Hickory NC
93 Royal Mason
Aledo TX
94 Sandy Fink
Dowling Park FL
95 Valma M. Bartlett
Oak Harbor WA
96 Joy L. Swope
Willoughby OH
97 Wendy Conroy
Denver CO
98 Royal Mason
Aledo TX
99 Mark Stokes
Great Neck NY
100 Mary I. Logan
Wellington New Zealand

STAGE PLAY SCRIPT WINNERS

1 Paul Mullin
Seattle WA
2 Hal Ackerman
Los Angeles CA
3 Khalil I. Sullivan
New York NY
4 Aoise Stratford
Ithaca NY
5 Paul J. Magliari
Stamford CT
6 Dee Kirkwood
Los Angeles CA
7 Paullette MacDougal
Edwards CO
8 Fred de Luna
West Linn OR
9 Nicholas Wardigo
Ardmore PA
10 Marvin Chernoff
Westlake Village CA
11 Don Hayes
Tampa FL
12 Neil Teague
Torrance CA
13 Giovanna Robinson/
Charles Knox Robinson
Palm Springs CA
14 Unknown
15 Fred and Anne Woodress
Muncie IN
16 Martha Humphreys
Huntsville AL
17 Sharon Harris
Lilburn GA
18 Marcia R. Rudin
New York NY
19 Cecelia I. Gaerlan
Berkeley CA
20 Max Branscomb
Bonita CA
21 Max Branscomb
Bonita CA
22 Michael Stockman
Boston MA
23 Bruce J. Graham
Winter Park FL
24 Jan Henson Dow/
Shannon Michael Dow
Woodbury CT
25 Susan Bennett Lobo
Thompsons Station TN
26 Mildred Trencher
New York NY
27 Ken Jennings
Jersey City NJ
28 Gloria Morris
Portland OR
29 Constance Gelvin
Colorado Springs CO
30 Barry Bradford
Chatanooga TN
31 Peter Nason King
Temple Terrace FL
32 John Williams
Tucson AZ
33 Michael Vukadinovich
Santa Monica CA

34 Simon Levy
Los Angeles CA
35 Heather Dexter
Seattle WA
36 Saul Greenblatt
Greenfield MA
37 Brenda Dee
Cape Canaveral FL
38 Don Orwald
Granbury TX
39 Joel Marlin
New York NY
40 Don Orwald
Granbury TX
41 Vanessa Yu
Plandome NY
42 Corinne Fleisher
Bradenton FL
43 David Wiener
La Jolla CA
44 Marcia R. Rudin
New York NY
45 Max Branscomb
Bonita CA
46 Saul Greenblatt
Greenfield MA
47 Jewel Seehaus-Fisher
Highland Park NJ
48 Tim Morgan
Merrimack NH
49 Walter J. Wojtanik
Sloan NY
50 James J. Delfiore
Cranston RI
51 Walter J. Wojtanik
Sloan NY
52 John Anastasi
Hollidaysburg PA
53 Jimmy Westmoreland
North Little Rock AR
54 Anthony Ingoglia
Westbury NY
55 Malvin Wald
Sherman Oaks OK
56 Lynne Kaufman
San Francisco CA
57 Lynne Kaufman
San Francisco CA
58 Rudy Makoul
Los Angeles CA
59 Lynne Kaufman
San Francisco CA
60 Unknown
61 Dean Taylor
Annapolis Royal NS Canada
62 Jane E. Smith/Lauri McKay Bevan
Willow Park TX
63 Monte R. Anderson
Aurora IL
64 Sindy Castro
Great Neck NY
65 Jim Potter
Hutchinson KS
66 David Reiner
67 Michael Lehto
Thunder Bay ON Canada

68 Sean Yokomizo
Moraga CA
69 Diana M. Ceres
Saint Helena CA
70 Alma Fuerte
71 Dean Taylor
Annapolis Royal NS Canada
72 Adam Amato
Manhasset NY
73 Monika Lee
London ON Canada
74 Antonio Donato
University Place WA
75 Alvin T. Ethington
Claremont CA
76 Roy Robbins
Cartersville VA
77 Marvin Chernoff
Westlake Village CA
78 Jeffrey Couillard
Columbia Heights MN
79 Leon Kaye
80 Don Orwald
Granbury TX
81 Craig Thornton
Watertown NY
82 Kathy Kafer
Pelham NY
83 Robert Ford
Fayetteville AR
84 Donn Wright
Green Lake WI
85 Alice Weiss
New York NY
86 Susan Surman
Winston-Salem NC
87 Faye Sholiton
Beachwood OH
88 Matthew Schneck
Brooklyn NY
89 Unknown
90 Edward Davison
Pine Mountain Club CA
91 Michael Brandt
Columbus OH
92 Saul Zachary
New York City NY
93 Sandra Hammack-Brown
Glenwood Springs CO
94 James J. Delfiore
Cranston RI
95 Lisa Rosenthal
96 Barrett O'Brien
Missoula MT
97 Gary L. Blackwood
Carthage MO
98 Don Warden
Missoula MT
99 Michael J. Vanderpool
Bradenton FL
100 Delvyn Case
Portland ME

84

TELEVISION/MOVIE SCRIPT WINNERS

1 Catherine Ross
Puyallup WA
2 Ona F. Lepard
Helena MT
3 Anne Toole
Los Angeles CA
4 Sharon Harris
Lilburn GA
5 Lynne Logan
Grove City OH
6 Bonnie Shepard Klein/
James Shepard
Miramar FL
7 Joe Siple
Rochester MN
8 Ona F. Lepard
Helena MT
9 Crystal Garrett
Stone Mountain GA
10 Cathy Stewart
Madison TN
11 Paul W. Tenny
Danbury NC
12 Daniel A. Chomistek
Medicine Hat AB Canada
13 Judi Guizado
Rancho Cucamonga CA
14 Jana Vandelaar
Key Largo FL
15 Steven Chang
Santa Monica CA
16 Gina Leone
Farmingville NY
17 Jana Vandelaar
Key Largo FL
18 Anne Toole
Los Angeles CA
19 Daniel A. Chomistek
Medicine Hat AB Canada
20 Sean Kelly
Prospect NS Canada
21 Melinda Stern
Agoura Hills CA
22 Sean Shealy
Littleton CO
23 Robert Ford
Fayetteville AR
24 Mike Dunn
Orange CA
25 Jana Vandelaar
Key Largo FL
26 Myra Donnelley
Portland OR
27 Niceole R. Levy
Pasadena CA
28 William Frank Georgi
Kalaheo HI
29 Everett T. Ruth
Newark NJ
30 Heidi C. Swanson
Pittsburgh PA
31 Deron Sedy
Seattle WA
32 Christopher L. Curran
Forest Hills NY
33 Robert A. Finan
Lakewood OH

34 Nick Vigorito Jr.
Brooklyn NY
35 James J. Tokarski
Kalamazoo MI
36 Nick Vigorito, Jr.
Brooklyn NY
37 Scott Gallaway
Bowling Green OH
38 Leon Cooper/Don Tait
Malibu CA
39 Judge Robert C. Van Auken
Fayetteville AR
40 Jacqueline Frazier
Venice CA
41 Jim L. Pope
Greeley CO
42 Theresa Wiza
Chebanse, IL
43 Cory Hollingsworth Ramirez
Sacramento CA
44 Joan Kufrin
Chicago IL
45 Christiana Miller
Los Angeles CA
46 Craig Clyde
Sandy UT
47 Don Kaufman/Jason Curtis
Estes Park CO
48 Mary Hargrove
Little Rock AR
49 Blake Casselman
Salt Lake City UT
50 Lee Kiszonas
San Francisco CA
51 Craig Clyde
Sandy UT
52 Sharon Gillespie
Austin TX
53 Jeffrey Poehlman
Los Angeles CA
54 Lisa Bardo/Kyle Creedon
West Melbourne FL
55 Paula Felps
Lewisville TX
56 Scott Kradolfer/Michael Lifshey
Burbank CA
57 Jim Hunnicutt
Orlando FL
58 Bob Camire
Manchester NH
59 Danielle Greene
Los Angeles CA
60 Cheryl S. Rosbak
Riverside CA
61 Bart Marshall
Raleigh NC
62 William Schrul
Philadelphia PA
63 Leslie Ann Sartor
Boulder CO
64 Arzhang Kamarei
New York NY
65 Lori Romero
Santa Fe NM
66 Susan Surman
Winston-Salem NC
67 Bob Canning
Petaluma CA

68 Nicholas Arena
Long Beach CA
69 Roger A. Hess
San Lorenzo CA
70 Roderick S. Chapman
Longwood FL
71 Sally Jane Kerschen-Sheppard
Suffern NY
72 Kevin Young
Saint Joseph MI
73 Craig Clyde
Sandy UT
74 Mark Daniels
Corbin KY
75 Robert O. Price
San Clemente CA
76 Christina Hamlett
Pasadena CA
77 Larry Michael Smith
Coffeyville KS
78 Susan Traxel
Dodge ND
79 Cassandra J. Taylor
Los Angeles CA
80 Cliff Gravel/Melody Groves/
Judy Avila
Albuquerque NM
81 Melanie Bates
Somerville NJ
82 Judge Robert C. Van Auken
Fayetteville AR
83 Spring Horton
Mountainair NM
84 Barry J. Brennessel
Seattle WA
85 Heather Goodwin
Brooklyn NY
86 Enrique R. Sanchez
Hialeah FL
87 Katherine Griffin
Los Angeles CA
88 Gayla Betts
Normal IL
89 Heather L. Jones
Asheville NC
90 Bernadette Y. Connor
Philadelphia PA
91 Harry Bauer
Chicago IL
92 Gayla Betts
Normal IL
93 Alisha Kloc
Saginaw, MI
94 Shavon L. Scott
Warren OH
95 Pat Ames
Mishawaka IN
96 Kyle Michel Sullivan
Los Angeles CA
97 John Conklin
Escondido CA
98 Linda Carol Anderson
Saint Louis Park MN
99 Ben Dubner
New Hyde Park NY
100 Barbara Grace English
Largo FL

85